BEAR'S MIDLIFE MATCHMAKER

FATED OVER FORTY

MEG RIPLEY

SHIFTER NATION

Copyright © 2022 by Meg Ripley
www.redlilypublishing.com

All rights reserved. Printed in the United States of America. No part of this book may be used or reproduced in any manner whatsoever without written permission except in the case of brief quotations embodied in critical articles or reviews.

This book is a work of fiction. Names, characters, businesses, organizations, places, events and incidents either are the product of the author's imagination or are used fictitiously. Any resemblance to actual persons, living or dead, events, or locales is entirely coincidental.

Disclaimer

This book is intended for readers age 18 and over. It contains mature situations and language that may be objectionable to some readers.

CONTENTS

BEAR'S MIDLIFE MATCHMAKER

Chapter 1	3
Chapter 2	14
Chapter 3	27
Chapter 4	37
Chapter 5	49
Chapter 6	60
Chapter 7	78
Chapter 8	86
Chapter 9	93
Chapter 10	107
Chapter 11	122
Chapter 12	136
Chapter 13	146
Chapter 14	158
Chapter 15	169
Chapter 16	179
Chapter 17	191
Chapter 18	203
Chapter 19	214
Chapter 20	225
Dean	235
Also by Meg Ripley	243

BEAR'S MIDLIFE MATCHMAKER

FATED OVER FORTY

1

"I can't wait to find myself some new man meat!" squealed the young woman to her friend as she flicked her hair behind her shoulder and marched into the room.

Carrie O'Connor held the door open, nodding, smiling, and introducing herself as the singles of Carlton, Oregon came streaming through. Well, not exactly streaming, but she had to admit there were far more people who'd decided to attend her Valentine's Day speed dating event than she'd anticipated. Jenna Sorenson, the marketer Carrie had met shortly after moving up from Sacramento, had insisted it would be a great way to get Carrie's name out into the community and help grow her clientele. Carrie had been doubtful at first, wondering if a relationship therapist should be hosting something so silly, but it was working so far.

The man-meat hunter notwithstanding.

"Come on in. You can fill out a name tag right over there, and we've got some hors d'oeuvres. We'll get started shortly." Carrie peeked out onto the porch of the old house and shut the door, rehearsing in her mind what she might say and how this might go. Her nerves were working overtime, even though she knew there was nothing to worry about. People would find dates, or they wouldn't. At the very least, it was a unique event that they weren't likely to find anywhere else in this small town.

A rap at the door had her turning back, and she blinked when she opened it. The man standing on the threshold had broad shoulders that strained at the leather of his jacket, but what held her attention the most were his stunning dark blue eyes.

"Uh, am I in the right place?" he asked. "Speed dating?"

Carrie blinked again and then got a hold of herself. She waved him inside. "Yes, of course. Come in. Just grab a name tag right over there." She slowly closed the door as she watched him walk over to the table she'd indicated. She expected certain types of people there: freshly divorced, permanently single, or socially awkward. It was hard to tell what category this guy might fall into, but if looks alone were the basis for dating prowess, then he didn't belong there at all.

Peeking out the sidelight to make sure she hadn't missed anyone else, Carrie moved over to grab her file off the top of the mantel. She'd printed out all the online surveys that everyone had submitted when they registered for the event, and she casually flipped through them. She was curious about what would make someone decide to come here tonight. That curiosity about people and how they dealt with relationships was exactly why she'd taken the career path she had, and she couldn't wait to see how it all turned out.

Glancing up to check out the name tags, she found a pair of eyes resting on her. It was Leather Jacket again, but he didn't turn away in embarrassment or try to pretend he was looking at something else. He let those deep sapphires linger on her face for a long moment before they traveled along the mantel, up to the trim work, and along the exposed beams of the ceiling. Hmm. Odd.

Checking her watch, Carrie decided she had a little more time before she needed to get started. She'd debated whether or not she should give anyone a chance to mingle and get to know each other before the official event began. After all, they were supposed to do that through a series of rapid-fire questions that would make them think on their toes, laugh a little, and perhaps be more honest when they didn't have a lot of time to think about the persona they hoped to put out into the world.

It was that thought, actually, that made her agree to this in the first place. Humans naturally only showed the best side of themselves to potential partners. They usually didn't come right out and talk about their bad habits or baggage. Sometimes, that left them twenty years down the road and wondering who the hell they'd actually married. She swiped the thought aside. It was time to get started.

But as she glanced around the room and prepared to get everyone's attention, Carrie's eyes instantly returned to Leather Jacket. While everyone else was watching or talking to each other, he studied the colonnade that divided the living room from the dining room. She rechecked her watch, but her curiosity was taking over. She walked over and stood on the other side of the half-wall as he ran his fingers down the column. "This one's not available for a date, I'm afraid."

If he was put off by her comment, he didn't show

it. Instead, he tapped his finger further down near the bottom of the column, where it rested on the pedestal wall. "It looks like these were replaced at some point. I have to wonder if it was merely a personal preference or some sort of structural issue. The house looks like it has good bones, though. And you've got an interesting mix of styles here. Mostly craftsman, but there are some nice rustic elements, too."

"Are you an architect or designer?" she asked. He didn't look like he sat behind a desk all day, not with a physique like that. His tag indicated his name was Pax, an odd one that she rolled around experimentally in her mind.

"Just a hobbyist, really. It's a nice house. A lot of potential. I'd love to get my hands on a place like this."

Carrie lifted a shoulder, trying not to let herself think about what it might be like to have his hands on her. How long had it been, anyway? Her best bet was to get things rolling before she let those thoughts get too far. "It's just the fastest thing I could rent when I moved up here. But we're about to get started."

"Sure thing."

Time suddenly began moving very swiftly.

Carrie quickly introduced herself, then explained how things would work. She'd arranged pairs of chairs in a circle around the room. The women would remain seated, and the men would rotate when the buzzer went off. "You'll have three minutes in each round to get to know each other. I suggest asking lots of questions, but it's fine if it turns into a more in-depth conversation. You'll see me moving around the room a bit, but I'm here if you need me. At the end, you'll have the chance to set up dates or exchange information. Everyone ready?"

The woman shopping for man meat giggled as she raised her hand. Her name was Sophie, written in swirling letters on her name tag with a tiny heart above the 'i.' "I know I am!"

"Let's get started, then." The men took their seats, and Carrie set her timer. As promised, she moved around the room a bit just to make sure things were going all right and that everyone was comfortable. She didn't want to invade anyone's privacy, but she wanted to ensure everything went smoothly. Plus, she was curious.

She leaned against a window as she overheard Pax and a woman in a slinky black dress. She'd let her hair fall down her back, and she'd put on far too much makeup. "So, do you like long walks on the beach?" she asked in a sultry voice.

"No."

"No? But they're so *romantic*," she countered, clearly offended that she should come to an event like this and find a guy who didn't agree with her every word.

He shrugged. "Not if you step on a jellyfish."

Carrie pressed her hand over her lips, and she was saved when the buzzer went off. "All right, gentlemen. Please move counterclockwise. There we are. And begin!" She reset the timer.

A younger couple seemed to be hitting it off, leaning toward each other with light in their eyes. Carrie moved past them and near Pax once again, though she pretended to be looking for something on the bookshelf.

"You're fire," purred a woman less than half his age. "What turns you on?"

Carrie rolled her eyes. It was clearly the girl's effort at being sexy, but it came off as desperate.

Pax wasn't bothered by it. "Watching a router bit perfectly shave off the edge of a custom-made tabletop."

The girl tilted her head in confusion, and Carrie bit her lower lip to keep from laughing.

On the next round, she leaned near the fireplace while she observed a couple who couldn't seem to find much of anything to say to each other. There were only so many guests there, and she again found herself near Pax. This conversation sounded like it was going a little better, though.

The woman had short dark hair. She looked age-appropriate, although Carrie knew these things weren't always cut and dried. "What do you do for a living?" It was a perfectly normal question.

"I'm a logger." Pax's reply was short and direct, although Carrie thought he could've expanded on the subject or asked her the same question in return.

"And in your spare time?" she pressed.

"Carpentry."

The woman gave an exasperated sigh. "Do you do anything that doesn't involve wood?"

Pax tapped the fingers of his left hand as he mentally ran through a list. "Nope."

It was difficult, but Carrie did her best to purposely avoid Pax for the next several rounds. She wanted to get a better idea of how things were going with the other participants, after all. It was natural for her to observe this process, paying attention to their body language, their chosen questions, and how they answered them. Carrie's sister had often compared her to a wildlife documentarian, breaking down the habits of wild creatures and their mating dances. She smiled to herself as she remembered that, thinking it wasn't entirely untrue.

On the final round, she saw that Pax was with Sophie. Carrie instinctively knew this was a match that could easily be perfect or volatile.

Sophie twisted a strand of her hair around her finger as she sat forward to show off her cleavage. "And what are *you* looking for in a woman?"

Pax shrugged. "Still trying to figure that out."

"Works for me," she said with a quirk of her eyebrow. "I've experimented with being a few different people."

"Whiskey or beer?" he fired back, ignoring her flirtatious comment.

Sophie pouted. "Wine, actually."

"You should come down to The Warehouse brewery. My cousin runs it, and I did all the woodwork in there. But they don't serve wine, so maybe you shouldn't."

That was a little harsh, though Carrie couldn't entirely blame him. Sophie wasn't there for anything serious. She'd announced her intentions as soon as she'd come in the door, and she hadn't bothered hiding the fact that she was only looking for a fling.

Some guys were probably thrilled with that, but not Pax.

The buzzer went off for the final time. "All right, folks! That's it. Please feel free to stay and chat if you'd like and exchange information. I've got a goodie bag for each of you when you leave." This had also been Jenna's idea. It had a brochure that explained all of her services, a coupon for a discount on her bestselling book, and some high-quality chocolate from Claire's Confections.

To her delight, several guests lingered for a bit. She saw cell phones come out as they traded numbers or social media handles, and she was pretty sure she even saw a calendar app or two pulled up. This had gone well!

When she turned to check on the refreshments, she spotted Pax. He hadn't talked to anyone afterward, and it bothered her. Sure, he'd been a bit blunt with a few of the women, but she had a hard time believing a hunk like him wouldn't end up with at least a date or two out of this. "Here's your goodie bag," she said, snatching one off the side table and placing it into his large hands. "How did things go?"

Pax turned those stunning eyes to her, slight amusement twinkling in them, and moved to the side as people started filtering toward the door. He moved a little further back when Sophie went by, though she'd latched herself onto some poor sap who was intrigued by her act and almost tripped over the threshold on his way out. "I just couldn't see myself in a relationship with anyone here. Except you."

"Oh." Carrie's ears rang as she stared into his ruggedly handsome face. Had that actually happened, or had she just imagined it? She gaped at him, completely unprepared. She'd thought she'd been primed and ready for anything that might've happened that night, but not this. Her cheeks burned, betraying the attraction she'd felt for him all night long.

As the last of the guests filtered out the door and onto the porch, their laughter drifting into the cold night air, Pax grabbed the timer from the table where Carrie had set it down. "Care to take a round with me?

2

Pax watched Carrie's lips open and then close again as she looked for the response she wanted. He felt his body instinctively leaning toward her even before she said anything, urging her to say yes. He wondered for a brief moment what the hell was wrong with him. He'd come to this stupid speed dating event because he'd felt like he should, not because he thought it'd be successful. The best thing to do would've been to leave when he'd had the chance and pretend that he'd never been there in the first place. Too late for that now.

"Um, sure."

"Why do women say that?" he asked as he moved back toward the pairs of chairs, selecting ones that were closest to the fireplace. A small blaze crackled inside, and he liked the craftsmanship of the mantel. It also provided him a place to set the timer down. "They don't just say yes or no. They say 'sure' and leave us guessing whether they really want to or not."

Carrie had pasted a carefully created expression on her face, one of complete neutrality. He'd already seen it on her several times that evening as she'd moved slowly and quietly through the room, leaving the scents of rose and vanilla trailing behind her. The expression broke with just the slightest tweak of an eyebrow, letting him know he'd gotten to her. "I think you're reading a little too much into that. The timer hasn't even started, and you're already asking questions."

"I see. You like to play by the rules." He hardly knew what he was doing as he set the timer and sat, daring her to turn and walk away from him. It was what Pax had expected when he'd shown up that night. In the forty-four years of his life, he had yet to meet anyone who made him quite that bold. Not that he was shy, not by any means, but he felt markedly different around her. His bear rumbled inside him, egging him on.

He could see that he was pushing her, too. There was the slightest bit of hesitation in her frame before she finally sat in the chair opposite him. Carrie didn't lean forward and show off her cleavage like Sophie had, nor did she flip her hair or caress her shoulders. She barely leaned her elbow on the arm of the chair as she stared him down. Pax had the distinct feeling he was being studied, but when the emerald green of her eyes rested on him, he wasn't sure he minded.

"I'll start," he offered, perfectly aware that he'd been a bit of an ass already. But he was committed now. He'd suggested it, and there they were. The other women hadn't been that much of a mystery to him. They were young and desperate for attention, or they were too used to rejection, or they would never find anyone good enough for them. Carrie was harder to instantly label that way. "Why are you running a speed dating event if you're single?"

Her eyebrow tweaked again, maybe a little more than last time. "Why not?"

"You can't answer a question with a question."

Her brows remained still this time, but the corner of her mouth edged up. She wasn't irritated anymore. She was amused at thinking she'd irritated him. "I just did."

"Fine, then I'll answer your question. Because you're too beautiful to be standing around watching everyone else get dates." Had he ever just come right out with a statement like that? Maybe, but this time it felt far more genuine than just some pickup line in a bar.

Her shoulders moved toward his. Barely. "Not *everyone*," she reminded him, tapping one finger on the table between them. "I didn't see you getting anyone's number before you left."

"Maybe I didn't find anyone worth my time." He could study her, too, and he found that he wanted to. Here was a woman he'd never met before, even though he'd lived in Carlton his entire life. That wasn't impossible, but it was odd that he should be so comfortable in a stranger's house, firing questions at her. He really did want to know more. "Until now."

Carrie turned her face slightly to the side, but her eyes stayed steadily on him. "Maybe you were too caught up in showing off how stubborn you can be."

"I'm not stubborn." He should've moved away from her at the jab. Pax knew that, yet he felt the distance between them slowly decreasing. His foot here, her knee there. Even his hands inched forward on the surface of the table, feeling the woodgrain beneath his fingertips.

Her lips curved up a bit more into what he could consider an actual smile. "You just proved that you are."

"What's your point?" he challenged.

Carrie turned her hands up to the ceiling, her fingers rolling back toward her palms like some benevolent goddess explaining to her devotee that the punishment they had coming was simply one they deserved and nothing personal. "That you sabotaged your speed dating session."

Pax now knew without any doubt that she *was* studying him. It hadn't been a figment of his imagination that she'd always ended up near him during the timed sessions. Carrie was trying to figure him out. Well, he'd have to wish her luck with that. No one else had figured him out yet, himself included. "Why would I do that?"

"You tell me."

Damn her. He didn't want to think about himself and why he'd gone there. In fact, he'd tried hard to forget it. Most of the drive over there, he'd been pumping himself up for the possibility of actually finding someone, but it hadn't worked. As soon as he'd seen the women arranged around the room, he'd known it was a bust. Pax didn't need those few minutes of rapid-fire questions to realize those women weren't what he was looking for. That was always the problem, though, wasn't it? Carrie was digging at him because she probably thought he'd be anything but truthful if he could help it. He could easily turn the tables on her by simply being honest. "Because I feel like it's time for me to settle down, and doing that with some vapid bimbo isn't my thing."

The moment of hesitation before she spoke again and her flushed cheeks were a victory as far as he was concerned. "You can always find someone else," she murmured.

Pax's eyes drilled deeply into hers. He could feel both sides of himself, bear and human, longing to get closer to her. He wanted to reach across the table and plunge his fingers right through those dark, curly locks to cup the base of her skull and see her look up at him with the same craving that he felt for her. "I think I just did."

She licked her lower lip, catching it in her teeth. "How do you know when you're attracted to someone?"

Was that a typical speed dating question or something she genuinely wanted to know? It didn't matter. Pax was in deep with her now. He would've told her anything in that moment. She'd reached straight inside him, so much so that he wondered if she could tell he was more than a mere human. "That weird little tickling in the back of my stomach," his lips said without his permission. "Like I'm feeling right now."

In a fraction of a second, he'd made his spontaneous fantasy come true. He brushed her hair away from the side of her neck as he pulled himself closer to her. Pax saw that velvety look in her eyes that he'd imagined, so exciting, yet so strangely familiar. He only gave himself a moment to study it, not wanting to see that softness go out of her eyes. His lips pressed against hers. The timer went off, a distant ping that didn't make any difference to him.

She'd been making efforts all night to be cool and distant, a neutral party while she expected everyone else around her to open up and be vulnerable. With the way she kissed him back, he knew now that it'd just been a wall, a thin shell she'd coated herself with. Her lips parted when his asked them to, and the slightest moan escaped her throat as his tongue slipped into the heat of her mouth. They were both pushing to their feet now, their bodies melding together as his free hand touched the curve of her hip beneath her dress. Pax found that he could hardly concentrate on his kissing as she pressed against him. Everything about her was soft, curving, and luscious. His nails scraped gently against the fabric, longing to get beneath it.

Carrie put her hands up on his chest, but she didn't push him away. He'd half expected it, considering how distant she'd tried to keep herself. Instead, her fingers splayed out and explored, slipping under each side of his jacket until she touched his shoulders. The move was subtly intimate, more than just a suggestion to take off his coat and stay a while.

It was a sign that he wasn't the only one who wanted to see where this was going.

Pax moved both of his hands around her hips to her lower back, daring to press himself against her so she could feel the effect she'd had on his body. He knew it was obvious even through the layers of fabric between them, and there was no point in trying to hide it. When he'd shown up that evening, he hadn't been sure of what he'd wanted. Now, he definitely did.

The deep reverberation of intrigue that rumbled across the back of her throat when she felt his hardness against her was all he needed. Pax bunched the skirt of her dress in his hands, slowly lifting it higher until he could get under the hem. Breaking their lip lock, he trailed kisses down the side of her neck and to her throat while he roved over the luxurious swelling of her backside. The scents of rose and vanilla were deeper where he touched his lips to her throat, hotter. Pax scraped his teeth against her skin, nipping for a moment before getting himself back under control and kissing once again.

But any part of that control he was still clinging to was about to be lost as she moved her hands down to his ribs and then further. She pulled at the material of his shirt, tugging it out of his waistband before she went for the buttons.

Now it was Pax's turn to make sounds with his throat. She wanted him; he and his bear both knew it. He didn't want to take his hands or lips off of her for a moment, and so they tumbled toward the rug laid out in front of the fireplace. There was no need to pull her down with him because she came willingly, the both of them leaving clothing in their wake. She kicked off her flats with ease as he lifted her dress over her head, and she went for his belt buckle. He felt his bear's frustration at the human propensity for clothing, but he couldn't deny the excitement of seeing what was beneath it. Carrie pushed his jacket and shirt from his shoulders until she could move her fingers across the broad planes of his chest, and his boots and pants came quickly after them.

He wanted to take her right then, this woman who intrigued him and challenged him and seemed to parse him into a million pieces with little more than a look. The way she lay there underneath him, with her lips barely parted and still plump from his kisses, she seemed much more innocent than a woman his age ought to be. The deep leafy green of her eyes, the same brilliant smattering color that he was used to seeing in the forest in the height of summer, pulled at him. Pax knew he could simply have what he wanted and be done with it, but Carrie made him want more.

Lowering himself alongside her, Pax pressed his body against her side. He turned her head toward him, smothering her questions with his lips. His right hand caressed the heavy globe of her breast, and he would've lingered there longer if he didn't have other places he wanted to visit. Pax trailed his fingers gently down the soft slope of her stomach, and when she trembled at his touch, he felt an answering echo within himself. He skimmed over the lush valley between her legs, teasing her as he stroked the sensitive skin on her inner thighs before he returned to it. He moved slowly at first, only increasing his pace as he could feel her desperation growing, her breaths coming in gasps between his kisses, her fingers pressing harder against the back of his shoulders. It was when her back arched up off the thick rug and she clung to him for dear life that he worked the hardest, eager to see what she was like when that hard shell of professionalism was not only cracked, but had completely fallen away. Carrie's face was pressed against his throat as she gasped, her body bucking as it tried to get closer to him.

Finally, Pax knew he couldn't wait any longer. He'd only been driving himself crazy as he'd brought her to climax, and both his bear and his human were getting hard to control. When Carrie let out a final cry against his throat, he swung his leg over her hips and pressed his hardness into her heat. The waves of her orgasm were still rippling through her body. Her hands were all over him, gliding up his arms, across his shoulders, and down his back. She felt incredible beneath him as he thrust, but it was when she dug her hands into his lower back and pulled him hard against her, letting out a trembling sigh, that he lost the last thread of control he'd been trying so hard to hold onto. He buried himself, hard and deep, taking, needing. She tightened and shivered around him, taking just as much as their moans echoed against the exposed beams of the ceiling.

The heat of the fireplace had almost been too much as they'd made love, but now it was a welcome sensation as the riot in his body subsided. He held her against him for a long while and watched her skin glowing in the firelight, a beautiful sight that he wouldn't mind studying for a long time. "I can stay if you'd like."

Carrie sucked in a breath, and her eyes widened as if she'd just woken up. "I'd probably better get to bed, actually. I've got appointments in the morning."

"Right." He dressed, but every action he took felt like the wrong one. He didn't want to get out of the house too quickly, or she'd think he was ashamed of what they'd done. He didn't want to hang around because then she'd think he wasn't going to leave, even though she'd asked him to.

Her dress was none the worse for the wear once she'd slipped it back on, though he could see the outline of her nipple through the fabric. He purposely lifted his gaze from it, but then his eyes lingered on her tousled hair that also wanted to remind him of what they'd just shared. She opened the door, pressing her shoulder against it.

Again he felt conflicted. If she didn't want him

there, why was she looking at him like that? "Call me?" he asked roughly.

Her tongue worked inside her mouth, making her lips and cheeks move, threatening to make him bring her back to the fireplace all over again. "Sure," she finally said.

As he fired up his truck and forced himself to drive off into the frosty night, he had to wonder if her hesitation had been genuine or simply another trick to make him show more of himself. Pax wasn't even entirely sure he cared, but even through her closed front door, he felt the pull of her as he drove away.

3

"And how does that make you feel?" Carrie kept her fountain pen moving as she listened to the Blackwells. Some of her clients had been happy to stay with her despite her move up to Oregon, feeling that sessions via video call would work just as well as coming to see her in person. She was listening, but she found herself focusing more on the way the pen laid down a satisfying wet line of ink. There was something she enjoyed about seeing it dry as she wrote, making something even as dull as taking notes much more fun.

"I just don't think he's fully considered what's at stake here," Victoria said, adjusting her glasses. She sat next to her husband and rested her hand on his knee, a good sign. Mrs. Blackwell was letting her husband know that she still cared for him even as she laid out her criticism of him. "Moving to another town is going to disrupt every aspect of our lives. I feel like he doesn't think it'll affect me at all because I work from home, but then we're changing schools, grocery stores, even coffee shops. It's just a lot."

Carrie glanced at the clock in the corner of her screen. "Looks like we're just about out of time. I suggest the two of you sit down separately to make a list of pros and cons about moving. Put everything down on paper that's important to you, even if you think it doesn't affect the other one. Go over it together and see where you get. I know you'd like to make this decision as soon as possible, so if you still need some help with it, just shoot me an email and I'll work you in for another session. Sound good?"

The Blackwells looked warmly at each other and nodded. "Yeah, I think we can do that," Robert agreed. "Oh, and congratulations on your book, by the way. I heard it hit the bestseller list."

"Thank you very much. I'll talk to you both soon." Carrie closed out the session, put her pen down, and leaned back as far as possible in her chair. That appointment had gone well on many levels, but she felt exhausted. Carrie knew it didn't have anything to do with the Blackwells, though.

It was Pax. She hadn't been able to get him out of her mind ever since she'd shut the front door behind him. She was even foolish enough to have peeked out her bedroom window after she'd gone upstairs, part of her hoping she'd still see his truck parked in front of her house. It was a ridiculous notion, she knew. Some hot guy like that—no matter how obstinate he could be if he wanted to—was actually interested in her. He'd probably come there hoping to find some Instagram model half his age, like most other guys in their forties seemed to want. Not a divorced mother of two grown children with stretch marks and cellulite on her ass.

Her face burned as she got up and went to the kitchen for another cup of coffee. Carrie hadn't thought about any of her insecurities in the moment. She'd been too focused on the way his hands felt against her body. And those eyes! They were downright soulful. It was only when she was alone again that she'd remembered she wasn't a young woman anymore, even though he'd made her feel like one.

"Stop it," she said to herself as she grabbed the hazelnut creamer from the fridge. "You've got another appointment coming up, and you need to pay more attention. Your old clients aren't going to keep doing long-distance sessions if they think you're spacing out."

A car drove by, and she leaned over the sink to glance out the window, wondering if her next client had arrived early. The woods near the back of the house cast long shadows up the driveway, with the bright morning sun sparking in between them. The car had gone on by, but something else caught her interest, something that hadn't been there the day before.

Taking a flannel from the hook near the door, Carrie marched out into the cool air. "If some nut put a political sign in my yard without asking—" She stopped short when she came around the other side of the sign. It'd been stuck into the ground with two slim metal spikes, and its cardboard body flapped in the breeze. She steadied it with her hand, but she could read it just fine. It was cold outside, but her cheeks were quickly heating up.

Back in the house, she called her landlord. While the phone rang on the other end, she took several deep breaths as she tried to remain calm, but it wasn't easy. "Mr. Morris, this is Carrie O'Connor."

"Calling when the rent's not even due yet? Sounds like this could be a busy day for me," the older man joked.

She couldn't share his humor. "I'm just wondering why there's a for sale sign in my front yard."

"Well, because the house is for sale," he replied.

Pinching the bridge of her nose and closing her eyes, Carrie reminded herself that she was trying to build a good reputation in this town. She'd been established in Sacramento, a place where there had literally been two hundred times as many people as there were in Carlton. This was the sort of small town where the rumor mill could make or break someone. "I understand that, in theory. I'm just a little thrown off, considering I just moved here and got settled in. Now, I'll have to move again?"

It was easy to imagine him shrugging his shoulders. Mr. Morris had been unflappable to a fault when he'd shown her the house, the sort of man who didn't get riled up about much of anything. "Well, you did say that the house was too big for one person."

"Yes. Yes, I did say that." She was sure as hell kicking herself for it now.

The landlord sighed. "I can see how this might be a little upsetting for you, but my daughter pointed out that it's time for me to downsize. I've sort of made a hobby of collecting rental homes over the years, but it's getting to be too much for me to keep up with. It was lucky enough that I managed to rent out your place to you. Most folks don't want to pay what a big house like that is worth, not in rent anyway."

"I see. Well, at least I know now. I don't suppose you have any other properties for rent that you aren't selling. Because, you know, I'll need a place to live." Carrie could hear the ice in her voice, but she didn't bother trying to thaw it. The man could've at least let her know what his plans were.

"No, I'm afraid not. I've got a few smaller places, but they're still occupied. I'll let you know if I hear of anything."

"Thanks." *For nothing, asshole,* she added mentally as she got off the phone. Carrie knew it was immature, and that wasn't the sort of thing a relationship therapist with a bestselling book that revolved around her career should be. Still, she couldn't help but feel jilted.

"Just look for the positive," she reminded herself as she picked up her coffee and headed back toward her office in the back corner of the house. "This place really is too big, even if I am using it for both a home and an office. It's got some charm to it, or it might if it was fixed up." Carrie slowed a little as she examined the wood trim and the old floors. She'd initially just seen it as a roof over her head, but maybe it could be something else.

Her cell ringing in her pocket jolted her back to reality. "Hi, Jenna. How are you this morning?"

"I'm great, thanks," the marketing consultant replied. "I'm dying to know how the speed dating session went! Was it a success?"

Carrie bobbed her head, looking for the right words. "You could say that. Everyone who signed up online showed, and I think most of them had a good time. I know at least a few were making plans to get together again."

If the event was supposed to bring a little satisfaction to some singles, then she'd definitely hit the nail on the head, given her tryst with Pax. A ripple of excitement ran through her body as she remembered his rough, magic hands. She couldn't remember the last time she'd given herself over to someone like that, especially a man she hardly knew. It'd paid off in spades, though. Carrie glanced over at the fireplace and thought she caught Pax's scent even now, something like cedar and sunshine.

"That's fantastic, but what I really wanted to know was if it was a success as far as getting your name out into the wild. Did anyone ask about your services?"

Carrie frowned. She'd been so focused on just pulling off the dating event that she hadn't thought all that much about marketing, at least not in an active way. Maybe she should've said more about herself or had her book on display. "I did make sure everyone got their goodie bags, and everyone seemed to have a good time."

"Good. I think we might be able to arrange some other functions that'll help you out as well. I've got a few things I'm brainstorming. I think it would really help people if they had a chance to meet you."

Pressing her lips together, Carrie looked around the room. Though she didn't want to think about him at all, she couldn't help but recall some of the things he'd mentioned. He said the house had great bones, and he'd admired the details with far more appreciation than she'd ever had. Carrie had simply wanted somewhere to live and work other than from the hotel room she'd checked into when she'd first arrived in Carlton, but maybe there was something more to this place. "I'd love to do another event of some sort, and I have something else I'd like to run by you as well."

"I'm listening."

Pulling in a breath, Carrie thought she might be completely insane for proposing this. The thing was, she was pretty sure Jenna would tell her if she agreed. That was what she needed right now: someone who would be completely honest with her. "This is a huge house, and it's really too big for me. You've seen it. I just found out a few minutes ago that it's for sale. Now, this is just a fledgling idea at the moment, but what are the chances I could make a successful bed and breakfast out of it?"

"Oh. *Oh.*" Jenna's second exclamation was one of enthusiasm. "You do have quite a bit of space there. It's out on the edge of town, so not too far from civilization, but also right near the wineries. And there aren't a lot of overnight accommodations here...."

Carrie could feel a sizzle of excitement bursting through her, one that didn't have anything to do with Pax this time. Well, he might've helped inspire it, but that was beside the point. "I could still keep my office in the back corner of the place like it is, so even if it's the off-season and I don't have guests, I'm making income."

"Which makes it a far more reasonable risk than a lot of people take on when they open a B&B," Jenna noted. "You've even got that separate driveway that runs around the side of the building, which means you can have your counseling clients come in through a different entrance from your guests."

"So you think it could work?" she dared to ask, wanting a direct answer instead of just hopes and dreams. It was wild. It was impulsive. It was absolutely not what she'd set out to do when she'd moved to Carlton, thinking she would just get a fresh start in a new town, one where she didn't have to think about her failed marriage or the fact that her children didn't need her anymore. This was a place that she'd been determined to make her own, and it was happening faster than she could've ever imagined.

"You know, I really do," Jenna said after a moment. "You've already got my brain churning out all sorts of promotional ideas for this. I'd say you just need to make sure it'll work out financially. I don't know how much work the house needs or how much your landlord is asking for it, but you'll want to look at more than just marketability."

"I'll do that. Thanks, Jenna. We'll be in touch again soon, I'm sure." When she got off the phone, Carrie practically ran through the house and back into the office. She grabbed a notepad and began scribbling down ideas, secretly hoping that her next client would be at least a little late.

4

"Beautiful day, isn't it?"

Pax glanced at Dean. "Yeah, I guess so."

"What do you mean, you guess so?" Dean pulled down the tailgate and hopped on it before he grabbed his thermos of coffee. "It's kind of hard not to notice when you're out working in it all day. It's chilly, but the sun is shining and it's not too muddy. That's more than we can usually ask for in February."

"Right." It was true enough if he'd bothered to think about it. Pax had been logging his entire adult life, working for his Uncle James at Thompson and Sons Logging. He was a nephew rather than a son, but that had never mattered. They were all family, and they were constantly looking out for the good of the clan. He lived, breathed, and ate sawdust. Sometimes literally. He could practically do the job blindfolded at this point in his life.

"What's the matter with you?"

Pax shook his head. "Nothing. I just didn't sleep well last night." That was simplifying the problem. He hadn't slept well, but this wasn't just a case of insomnia. It was Carrie. He'd walked into her house yesterday for that damn speed dating night. He'd done it because he thought he should, even though it wasn't going to make any real difference. At least if he was making an effort to find a mate, that should count, right? That should make fate wake up and remember that he wasn't supposed to be a bachelor forever. He was mostly happy, but in the back of his mind, he was always wondering if he'd met her and had been too preoccupied to notice.

Despite his interest in finally settling down, Pax honestly hadn't expected to find anyone worthwhile at the event. He hadn't, at least not when it came to the women who'd drilled him for three minutes about mundane things before moving on to the next guy. He could've predicted just about every second of that grueling experience.

But Carrie? She wasn't anything he'd expected at all. She was smart. That much he'd been able to tell right away. It was something about the way she carried herself, her eyes, the way she spoke—just all of it. And even though she'd done her best to hold it back, she was undeniably sexy. She'd tried, but he'd found the primal creature hiding inside of her, the one she kept at bay. In that sense, she wasn't much different from him.

He'd gone home as she'd asked, but he hadn't liked it. Pax steeled his jaw as he slugged back his coffee. An edginess had settled into his bones as soon as he'd stepped out onto Carrie's porch. At first, he'd thought it was because he'd enjoyed himself and wanted to stay, hoping for a second round. As his headlights burned through the darkness of the night, though, he felt like he was leaving a vulnerable member of his clan unprotected. He'd lain in bed, tossing and turning so much that the fitted sheet had popped off the corners of the mattress. He'd just had the most gratifying sex he'd had in a long time, yet he couldn't sleep? That wasn't right, and he wasn't sure what to think about it.

"Don't sit for too long," James Thompson said with a grin as he joined them, grabbing his thermos.

"We've got a lot of work ahead of us today, and it's not like we're going to run out anytime soon."

Pax capped his coffee and lifted his chin at his boss. "Does that mean what I think it means?"

"You bet!" James clapped him on the back and laughed. "We got the Copeland contract!"

"Hey, that's great," Dean enthused. "I didn't think they were going to make a decision on that for a while yet."

James put his hands up in the air as though their logging operation couldn't help being as spectacular as it was. "I know he was hesitant to make a decision, but I kicked it over the edge. I think it all boiled down to our methods. I was able to get with some of the other landowners we've worked with in the past. Since we've been select cutting and doing such a good job of leaving as much of the land intact as possible, he was impressed with the quick recovery. Mr. Copeland said he wouldn't even know the land had been logged."

"I'm not surprised." Pax looked around as he fished a sandwich out of his bag. It was good work and satisfying. He enjoyed getting out in the woods no matter what form he was in, and there was something gratifying about choosing the trees that were just right for lumber. They fell slowly at first, almost as though the tree was deciding if it would allow itself to be cut, but then there was that final thump to the ground. It was a destructive process, but the Thompsons always tried to leave the land they worked as undisturbed as they could. Many of their clients probably didn't realize it was just as important to them that the land stay as pristine as possible, and it was paying off. Pax was glad to have this project on the horizon. He'd need plenty of work to keep himself distracted from Carrie.

"I hate to break the good mood," Evan said as he walked up, wiping his hands on a rag, "but the skidder's down."

James whipped his head around to look at the operator. He was another cousin of Pax's and part of the clan, one who had come into the logging business more recently but who had proven himself to be an excellent machine operator. "How could that be? It was just fine yesterday."

Evan shook his head. He wiped the last of the oil off his hands before he reached up and rubbed his shoulder. "That's why I've been crawling around trying to figure it out. It's a hydraulic hose."

Pax noticed a vein bulge from his uncle's temple.

"I thought you just went over all those about a month ago and replaced the ones that needed it."

"Sure did," Evan replied. "But there's a big ass split on one of the main lines. Unfortunately, I've already called the shop, and they don't have any in stock. It's going to take a couple of days to get anything in."

"Shit." Dean slapped his leg. "How's that for timing?"

"Doesn't exactly seem like a coincidence if you ask me," James said quietly. He rubbed a knuckle along his jawline. He was a man who took his business very seriously. Their clan had been working the woods for a long time, and he'd seen a lot. "We get the Copeland contract, and then a hydraulic hose bursts? Sounds like the Ballard boys have been sniffing around our operation."

"I don't know about that." Pax swallowed, saving the other half of his sandwich for later. He hadn't been all that hungry, though he certainly should've been after staying up all night and then working hard all day. "I know we don't have a good relationship with the Ballards, but they haven't said or done anything to us in a long time. I mean, when was the last time they started a fight?"

"Today, apparently," James snapped.

Pax leveled his gaze at his uncle. He knew James had a bit more of a temper than he did, and he tended to fly off the handle a little too quickly. Hell, when Pax's cousin Chase had decided to leave the logging industry, James had treated it like the end of the world. It had eventually worked out for the best, and Chase's brewery was doing well, but the accusation toward the Ballards still seemed like an overreaction. "I think we'd better be one hundred percent certain before we accuse them of anything. We don't want to start something without a good reason."

Evan sighed. "I think there very well may be a reason. I've been working on these machines for a while now, and I know what it looks like when a hose is busted. This one was cut."

"You're sure?" James asked, his voice a hard edge.

"Absolutely."

Pax cursed under his breath. "Would they even have time to know about the contract? If you just found out today?"

"You know how this town operates," James pointed out. "The wind blows rumors around like leaves. Besides, our feud with them goes a long way back. I wouldn't be surprised if they've just been sitting around waiting for a chance like this."

Pax wasn't so sure. He'd even seen some of the

Ballards in town a couple of weeks ago, and they hadn't been the least bit aggressive. It made Pax wonder if there was still any real conflict between the clans at all. That didn't mean he would argue with his uncle, though. "I'll bring it up to Chris and see what he says." Their Alpha tended to be calm and collected, and he wouldn't take any action before thinking this through.

"In the meantime, what do you want us to do?" Dean asked.

James looked up at the late winter sky. "We could still cut plenty, but we're supposed to get rain soon. I don't want to fall behind and have anything get waterlogged or rot on us. We've worked hard for the reputation we have, and I'm not going to sacrifice that. Evan, get the ball rolling on fixing the skidder, and order some backup parts while you're at it. I don't want us to get caught with our pants down again. You boys can take the rest of the day off, and I'll get some things done at the office. I'll let you know as soon as we're up and running again."

After packing up, Pax was back in his truck and heading through town toward his place. He hadn't planned on having a day off, but he sure as hell wasn't going to spend it sitting around watching TV. As it was, his mind was already drifting back to

Carrie. He wondered what she was doing. The website where he'd signed up for the speed dating event had listed her as a relationship therapist. Pax could imagine her sitting in a big, cushy office, her curls pulled back into a crisp bun as she listened to a couple hash out their problems. Of course, the fantasy quickly turned into one of his own as she let down her hair and revealed that other side of herself, the one that he'd gotten a glimpse of the previous night, like peeking through a heavy wooden door and finding a lush paradise on the other side.

Without intending to, he realized he was on the same road as her house. He slowed down as he saw it, once again admiring the craftsmanship. The place had been built back when people viewed their homes as art, something to show off to their neighbors. They spent the money hiring men like him, men who did more than just build a roof and install windows. They left the rafter ends exposed, often hanging beyond the eaves, and added ornamental pieces just for show. Extra stickwork had been put in under the gabled dormers, and the porches were held up by wide columns and decorative walls. The Craftsman style had been one of Pax's favorites for a long time. It wasn't as dainty and fussy as Victorian homes, and it carried the art of woodwork with a stateliness he admired.

What he noticed right now, however, was an older man standing in the front yard. He was using a small hammer to tack something down into the ground with gusto. Pax felt a bubble of excitement when he saw what it was, and he pulled over and rolled his window down. "You're selling this place?"

"If the damn sign will stay in the ground with this wind," the man grumbled, putting one final stroke on the sign before rubbing a hand through his gray beard. He looked up at Pax with limpid, hound dog eyes. "You interested?"

Pax lifted his gaze to the house. He'd noticed Carrie when he'd first walked in. She'd been impossible to miss. But the backdrop of that gorgeous house was quite fascinating on its own. He jotted down the number on the sign. "I just might. I'll let you know."

He headed home, eager to get his hands busy in his workshop. Pax had built a bit of a reputation for himself around town with his woodworking skills, and he often had a project or two going on the side. He'd helped remodel his cousin Chase's brewery, The Warehouse, and then again when the place had burned. Now, he had the beginnings of a hall tree for an older woman out on the edge of town and a convertible coffee table for a couple who was working from home a lot now that they had children in the picture. He flicked on his dust collection system and let the muffled sound of his saws and routers work through his mind as he tried to decide.

It was a beautiful place, the sort of home that people bought and held onto. Pax had often regretted that his house was rather plain, with no original hardwood floors or decorative trim around the windows. Sure, he could put those in himself, but it wouldn't be the same as something that had already been around for a hundred years. And it felt like putting lipstick on a pig. The minimalist style of his little place just wouldn't look right if he embellished the hell out of it simply for the sake of doing so.

The more he thought about it, the more he could feel his excitement growing. Carrie's house was screaming for help. He'd noted all the woodwork and how it had been neglected over the years. It needed to be sanded and restained. There were probably a few pieces that should be replaced entirely. The floor required work, and the kitchen could use a thorough update. Pax didn't need a home that big, but he could probably turn quite a profit on it after he did all the work himself.

It was impulsive, but he knew he could pull it off without a hitch. Before he could talk himself out of it, Pax turned off his table saw, got out the number, and called.

5

"So, how's Oregon? Have you met any cute guys yet?"

Carrie was glad this call wasn't a video chat. Alisha would've known right away if she could've seen her sister's face. They just knew each other that well. It wasn't as though Carrie was in the habit of keeping secrets from her sister, who was practically her best friend. But it was a little harder right now because she didn't exactly know how to explain Pax. "A few," she finally admitted, "but you know that's not what I'm here for."

"Oh, come on," Alisha teased. "No single woman in her right mind would move to a new area and not at least *think* about what kind of possibilities there might be. Even a therapist," she added pointedly.

"I know. I've actually got something even bigger that I'm thinking about diving into."

"Tell me! Oh, hang on." Alisha put her hand over the phone, muffling whatever was going on in the background.

Carrie could tell she was talking to one of her kids. Her sister had started her family much later in life than Carrie had, so she was still dealing with packing school lunches, helping out on field trips, and getting stuck with fundraisers. Carrie had enjoyed all of those things as they were happening, but she didn't miss them now. Cameron and Catherine would call her if they needed her, but they also had each other since they'd decided to attend the same college.

"Okay, sorry. Now tell me everything!" Alisha said when she came back.

Carrie stood in the middle of her living room. She closed her eyes, hoping that her announcement was going to go over as well as she'd hoped. She'd been thinking about it all day, and she had yet to see a downside. "I'm thinking about opening a bed and breakfast!"

A long pause made her glance at her phone screen to see if Alisha was still there. "Really?" Alisha finally asked.

"I know it's a little out of the blue," Carrie admitted. She opened her eyes and began pacing the room, carefully avoiding the fireplace. She'd turned up the thermostat instead of putting any logs on the fire that night. It would've been warm and atmospheric, but it would've made her think about Pax. Again. "The thing is, I'm renting this house that's way too big, and the guy has decided to sell it. I can make use of the space, so it won't feel like I'm just rattling around inside a giant box all the time. There aren't a ton of other places for sale or rent around town, so it'll save me from having to look for something new and reestablish where my practice is all over again."

"Just make a peanut butter sandwich. Dinner's running late. Sorry, Care. I'm listening. I'm just surprised, that's all. I didn't think you were into the hospitality thing."

"Well, no," Carrie admitted. "Like I said, it's just an opportunity that's fallen into my lap. I spent quite a bit of time talking about it with my marketing consultant, Jenna. We went over all sorts of ideas. I'll keep my office around the back where it is right now, so my clients will have some privacy when they come to see me, even if there are guests at the B&B. We even talked about putting together getaway packages for couples who want to work on their relationship and vacation at the same time."

"Do people really do that?"

Carrie tipped her head to the side. "I wrote a whole chapter about just that sort of thing in my book. 'Getting Away While Getting in Touch.' People can benefit from a change of scenery, not to mention taking away all the household burdens that weigh us down."

"Right. Sorry. I guess that does make sense, especially if your consultant thinks so. To be honest, I'm kind of surprised one of those exists in a small town like that. No, honey. We don't jump on the furniture."

"The other benefit is that I'll have some space here in case anyone wants to visit," Carrie added. It was a far more selfish justification for her little guesthouse idea, but it was one of the ones she liked the most. "You know, if Cam and Cat are on break from school and they want to come up, then I can make sure I have room for them. Or you guys."

"Aw. That sounds nice. I miss you, Carrie."

Her heart panged a little as she glanced out the window. It was starting to get dark, and the heavy amount of trees on the property meant that it got darker a little faster. She'd never been afraid of the dark, but it did make her feel a little more lonely. Especially right now. "I miss you, too. I'd love for you guys to come up and see the place. I mean, it needs some repairs. I'd have to redo the bathrooms and the kitchen for sure, and I'll be spending all my spare time painting and decorating if I actually want to follow through with this, but I think it's going to be amazing."

"I'm sure it will. Hang on a second." Alisha didn't say anything for a moment as the general chaos of her house died down behind her, and the distinct shutting of a door suggested she'd snuck off to the master bedroom for a moment of privacy. "It sounds great, Carrie. If there's anyone who can run two businesses out of their home, it's you."

"But?" Carrie sensed the hesitation in her sister's voice, and she felt the weight of it over her shoulders like a heavy blanket. It wasn't that she needed Alisha's approval for this, but she wanted it anyway. She wanted someone to feel that excitement with her.

"It's not really a *but*," Alisha hedged. "It's just that it all sounds very practical. That's very *you,* and don't think I've forgotten that for a moment. Not even five hundred miles between us will make me forget that. But usually, when people get divorced, they do something wild. They go out and get crazy. You never did that, and I've often worried that you'll regret not getting that out of your system."

Carrie let out a little snort of laughter. She couldn't help it. "I never really felt justified in doing that, not with kids at home. And I've been divorced for years now, Al. I'm over all that."

"Are you sure?"

"Don't you think I'd know?" Carrie felt her stance was justified, both because only she could know what she wanted and because she'd spent most of her adult life studying this sort of thing. For reasons she couldn't quite explain, she'd always been interested in the way people interacted. Even as a young child, Carrie noticed relationships that seemed equal on the surface weren't always that way underneath. Her parents were still married and got along well, but she had friends whose parents stayed married even though they screamed at each other every night. There were some folks who were the rudest to those they claimed to love, yet sweet as pie to the cashier at the grocery store. This observation had created a thirst for knowledge that she was never quite able to quench. Why do people act the way they do?

"And actually," she continued, knowing Alisha

wasn't going to be completely satisfied with her answer, "buying a massive house and turning it into a bed and breakfast *is* a little wild. I'm going to be investing pretty much everything I've made off my book."

"I guess that is pretty risky. You're not going to get yourself in financial trouble, though, are you?"

Carrie smiled. Alisha had gone from urging her to go wild to worrying about her. It was only because the sisters cared about each other so much, and she loved Alisha all the more for it. "I've still got a steady income. I have quite a few clients that were happy to do distance appointments, so I didn't have to lose everyone from Sacramento. I'm starting to see some new faces trickle in, too, and then I have Jenna to help me keep connecting with people here."

Of course, that effort was exactly what had brought Pax into her life. She wondered if she should call him. Did he want her to, or had he just said that so he wouldn't seem rude? Carrie didn't know him well enough to be sure.

"If this is something you really want to do, then you know I'm behind you one hundred percent," Alisha said. "And I guess I can't worry about you sowing your wild oats too much. You probably wouldn't have moved to the middle of nowhere if you were still stuck in the same place as you were five years ago."

"True enough. I'm still trying to figure out exactly how to make my life my own, but I'm getting there."

"Hang on, baby! Listen, I've got to go. But I'm glad you called, and I can't wait to hear how all of this goes. Keep me updated, okay?"

"I will. You're my favorite sister."

"And you're mine!"

It was their little inside joke since they were each other's only sisters, but it never got old. Carrie hung up, but she kept her phone in her hand. Was she actually going to do this? She'd already told someone about it, which made it more real. Not that Alisha would hold it against her if she changed her mind. It was a lot of money, but what did she have to lose? She didn't have kids at home to support. She had enough income to live off of even if no one wanted to stay at her little inn. Jenna seemed to think it was a good idea, and she had tons of reviews online saying how much she'd helped other small businesses grow. Carrie dialed.

"Hello." Mr. Morris sounded tired.

"It's Carrie O'Connor. I'd like to buy the house."

"Which one?"

"The one I'm living in," she reminded him.

"Right. Oh, right. Sorry. It's been a long day. Um, I have to tell you, I already got an offer for the asking price."

Her jaw slackened, and her heart dipped down into her shoes. She hadn't imagined that a simple little sign in the yard would've been noticed by anyone so quickly. Was the housing market that hot around there? She was no real estate expert, but she'd already seen firsthand how difficult it was to find a decent place.

"Hello? You still there?" Mr. Morris asked.

"Yes. I'm just a bit surprised."

"Okay, well, the buyer didn't say whether he meant to keep it as a rental house or not. Everyone around here knows that it's one of my rental properties since I've got so many of them. I guess you could consider this a notice from me, but you might not want to pack your boxes just yet until you get a chance to talk to the buyer."

As Mr. Morris rambled on, Carrie thought back to her conversation with Alisha. Her sister was right: Carrie was always practical. She'd hardly ever done anything spontaneous. Hell, that had been one of Brian's complaints about her. Carrie wasn't *fun*. She liked routine, her studies, and peace and quiet. She knew Brian didn't appreciate how her hips had widened after having their kids, and how breastfeeding, gravity, and time had transformed her 34-Bs into 38-Longs.

But there was nothing to hold her back now, including Brian. Her royalties and her fees continued to come in. Her book money was better used as an investment than piddling it away in rent. No, wait. That was the practical side coming through again.

"I'll give you ten thousand over the asking price."

There was a stunned silence on the other end of the line. "You're sure?"

"Yes." She said the word firmly, both to convince him and herself. She couldn't back out of this now. It would mean she'd have to keep thinking about it, hemming and hawing over the pros and cons. Carrie had only been at that for a day, but it was already exhausting her.

"Well, all right then," Mr. Morris said in his slow, casual way. "I'll take it before you change your mind. But I sure hope you get hopping on your financing and your paperwork. I don't want this to turn into a bunch of haggling."

"I will, Mr. Morris. You have a good evening." She ended the call, left in the silence of the home.

Carrie filled it with a shriek of excitement as she ran into her office to grab a notebook and her fountain pen. It had been exciting to know that she could finally live her life for herself once her kids were on their own. It'd been thrilling to move to a new part of the country, one that she could truly call her own. But now, knowing she was about to make a bigger change than she'd ever imagined, she was exhilarated. Her hand could hardly keep up with her brain as she started making lists. A page for each room, and everything that needed to be done. Paint, rugs, light fixtures, new doors, trim, flooring. She had yet to decide what sort of theme she would go for, and she'd doubtlessly be up all night searching for ideas on her phone, but that was all right. She was about to take a risk. Finally.

6

SATURDAY SHOULD'VE BEEN A GOOD DAY FOR PAX. HE wouldn't have minded getting out into the woods, but of course, that was still on hold until Evan could get the hose fixed. Though he liked his job, Pax enjoyed his workshop even more. There, he could work on the projects of his choosing. He could cut, sand, and stain to his heart's content, sometimes while listening to music, and other times, just enjoying the thrum of his machines. He worked at his own pace, creating something artful and useful out of boards and logs that wouldn't look like much to anyone else. In there, he could lose himself in the rhythm of the work, like a meditation for the mind and hands.

His phone rang, vibrating in his pocket, and he

flicked off the sander. As he checked the screen, he realized that he'd been secretly hoping it would be Carrie, finally calling to see if they could have another romp by the fire. The number was familiar, but he was pretty sure it wasn't hers. "Hello?"

"Yeah, this is Dane Morris. I just thought I'd let you know that I got another offer on the house, one that's ten thousand over what I was asking."

"You're shitting me."

"Afraid not. I could hardly believe it myself. Figured it'd linger around on the market for a while since it needs so much fixing up."

It sure did, and he'd been looking forward to doing it. Pax had been eager to dive into the house and see what he could really do with it. There would be bits and pieces of history that would have to be thrown away, but he'd already gotten himself excited about tearing into it and seeing where he'd be able to leave his own mark for future generations to find.

Then there was the idea that he'd be able to use the house as a distraction from Carrie. Even without talking to or seeing her again, Pax knew nothing could ever work between them, yet his mind had refused to let go of her. Even his inner bear had picked up the idea of her and had run away with it, keeping it clamped in its jaws and huffing at him stubbornly. Maybe it was just as well that the house went to someone else. Working there wouldn't really be a distraction for him, because Pax knew he'd only think of her every time he walked through the door. Would he still smell the heated perfume of her skin?

"Thanks anyway," he said a bit too harshly. "I appreciate you letting me know." He hung up without bothering to ask who it was or if he could try to outbid them. He'd thrown his hat in the ring, but that didn't mean he was going to throw everything else after it.

Moody and sour, he went back to his work, but it didn't soothe him like it usually did. Pax knew it wasn't simply the house. Sure, that was a part of it, but it was more than that. He checked his phone again, but there hadn't been any further calls or texts. He hesitated, his finger on the power switch of the drill press. So he'd missed out on the house, but what about its current occupant? Where would she go when the new buyer took over? What if she moved out of town and he never saw her again?

He dusted off his clothes and grabbed his keys. This was a stupid idea. Pax knew it. She was a human. He was a shifter. She, like most humans, probably had no clue that people like him even existed. If she did, it would crack that hard shell of hers into pieces so small, she'd never be able to put them back together.

Besides, even if she actually knew what he was, she wasn't right for him. If they were supposed to be together, they would've stayed together that night. She would've wanted him to, no matter what her work schedule was like the next day. And he would've insisted. The proof of them not being mates was right there in front of him, but then again, he'd pretty much given up on finding The One. Of course, he didn't need her to be right. He just needed someone.

Shit. He was arguing circles around himself.

It was too late to continue the dispute when he pulled up in front of her house. Mr. Morris must have come along and pasted a big red 'SOLD' tag on top of the sign because it mocked him as it flapped happily in the breeze. Fine. Let it be sold, but at least he still had the chance to figure out just what it was about Carrie that had reached inside him and made him so unsettled.

Annoyed with himself, mostly for being so annoyed in the first place, Pax marched up onto the porch and rang the bell. His throat tightened as he waited. There was music inside, but he couldn't tell what song it was. He stuffed his hands in his pockets and realized he had no idea what the hell he was going to say. He couldn't exactly be upset with her for not having called yet. It'd only been a couple of days, and neither he nor any of his single friends would've acted that quickly. He hadn't left anything behind that he'd needed to retrieve. Shit.

Her footsteps sounded on the old floor just a moment before the knob rattled and the door opened. She stood there wearing a pair of faded but well-fitted jeans that tapered at the ankle, just above the fuzzy socks she wore on her feet. Though her eyes were beautiful as they were, her green cable knit sweater made them even brighter than usual. Pax suspected that was also due to the glass of champagne she held in her hand. Her head tipped slightly to the side as she smiled at him. "Hey."

"Hey. I, uh, I was just driving by and saw that the house sold. That must've happened pretty quickly. I just thought I'd check in with you. That's got to be a little bit upsetting." Pax didn't like the way he sounded. He could hear the nerves in his voice, and that wasn't like him.

"Actually, it's pretty exciting." She smiled a little wider as she stepped back and held the door open. "Come on in and I'll tell you all about it."

He did as she asked, and he felt a deep sense of

satisfaction stirring from within him as soon as he crossed the threshold. His bear, which had been tense and restless for the last couple of days, finally relaxed. All the bad moods he'd drifted in and out of felt like little more than a bad dream.

"Can I get you a glass of champagne?" She moved toward the dining room, where she fetched another glass out of the built-in china cabinet.

To follow her, he had to walk past the fireplace. His blood thrummed in his veins as he imagined what it'd be like to pull her toward him right now, her mouth tasting of the sweetness of her drink as he kissed her, his hands buried in her hair or sliding those jeans right down those luscious hips. "What are you celebrating?" he asked instead.

"My purchase of the home," Carrie replied with a grin as she handed his glass to him.

He barely moved his hands as she clinked her glass against his and took another sip. "*You* bought it?"

"Sure did. I had to put in a little extra cash, since there was already an offer on the place, but I'm trying to convince myself that it was worth it." The tip of her tongue slipped between her teeth as she smiled again.

Pax hadn't even had a drink yet, but he was

already feeling quite disoriented. This news itself had thrown him off. Then there was the fact that the champagne had already softened her some. She wasn't the therapist he'd met two nights ago, the distant observer who watched everything like she was going to write a column about it for *National Geographic.* Neither was she gasping and writhing in his arms, but somewhere in between. "I'm sorry if I'm a little surprised. I just didn't realize you were interested in it."

She lifted one shoulder as she bobbed her head. "I didn't quite realize it either until the opportunity came up. I'm going to turn it into a bed and breakfast, actually."

He opened his mouth to reply, but nothing came out. Instead, his eyes roved to the details he hadn't seen when he'd been there before. The speed dating event had been confined to the front room, which meant he'd only seen the gorgeous woodwork around the mantel and the recently refinished entryway. Now he saw the window trim in the dining room that'd been painted over numerous times without any sanding in between, with so many layers of latex that it was stretchy and soft. Then there was the wallpaper, which was peeling slowly down from the ceiling. The cabinet Carrie had taken the glass from was in mostly good shape, but the hinges were starting to give out on one side, and the whole thing would benefit from a good sanding and staining. "That could be a lot of work," he said hesitantly.

"I know," she replied, not seeming to be upset or offended in the least by his comment. Carrie set aside a rather fancy-looking pen and picked up the notebook underneath it. "I've actually been spending most of the day deciding what I want to do with every room in the house. I'm sure there are going to be some things I don't anticipate, but it's a start."

His tongue was sticking to the roof of his mouth, so he took a sip of the champagne. It was light and sweet, and he hoped it would help him relax a little, too. Did Carrie have any idea that he'd put a bid in on the house as well? She didn't seem to. That alone made him feel a bit better. He couldn't say that he minded losing out as much if it was to her. "Can I see?"

"Sure." Carrie flicked the notebook open, displaying a page that said, 'Dining Room.' The handwriting was remarkable, and the ink was the same dark green as her sweater and her eyes. "I'm assuming the light fixture in here probably needs to be replaced, and of course, the whole room needs to be painted. I like the wallpaper, but I think I'd rather paint than deal with replacing it. Then there's the floor."

Pax ripped his eyes away from the carefully crafted list. "It looks like it's in pretty good condition for its age."

"Sure, what you can see of it." Carrie set everything down to free her hands while she pulled out two of the dining chairs and flicked back the rug, which took up most of the room. She revealed a large patch of hardwood that wasn't even the same color as the border that could be seen around the edges. "Not so great."

He let out a small laugh. "It looks like someone only refinished what they knew would be seen."

She shrugged as she put everything back. "I knew about it when I moved in, and I didn't think much of it since I knew I'd put the rug there anyway. But now that I'm going to be having guests, it seems like I should get it fixed up."

"Not interested in marketing it as charming and quaint?" he teased.

"Oh, it's quaint all right. Come here. I'll show you something." Notebook and champagne in hand, she led him through the next doorway and through the kitchen. She stepped into a corner that was pitch black for a moment, but then a swinging lightbulb in what turned out to be the pantry turned on. Carrie was grinning as she pointed to the door trim around the pantry's entryway. "Come here. Look at this."

It was one thing to stand on opposite sides of a dining room table, but now he had to squeeze in next to her. His flannel seemed to like the material of her sweater, clinging to it as he stood next to her, and he could feel her breath on his arm. Pax felt his bear stirring once again, but not in the same way that it had been over the last few days. It'd been restless and angry, demanding that he go back to her house. Now it was much clearer about exactly *what* it wanted, and he clenched his teeth together to drive it back down for a little while.

"Right here, look. Whoever owned this place a long time ago had measured all their children here in the doorway. I did the same thing with my kids when they were little." She pointed to the carefully marked lines, dates, and names, running her finger over them reverently.

"You have kids?"

"Mmhm. Twins, but they're grown now."

"I didn't realize…"

She flicked her ring finger casually. "I'm

divorced." Her tone was dismissive, not reflecting the pain or regret that usually came along when people said such things.

Her face was close to his now, and it was impossible not to study her profile. Pax longed to run his fingers down her soft jawline and caress his thumbs over her cheekbones. The lines on the outside corners of her eyes only emphasized how bright and beautiful they were. The effect was heightened by the pleasant flush of her cheeks when she mentioned her children. Somewhere along the way, someone had decided they didn't want her anymore. That was impossible for him to believe.

"And then look up here," she said, not noticing his attention nor bothered by her mention of her past relationship. "Ma and Pa measured themselves, too. I can just see these three little kids telling their parents that they had to do it with them. I know there's a lot that needs to be replaced around here, but not this part. This I'm keeping."

A zing of electricity was flowing through Pax, one that he knew wasn't inspired by her interest in holding on to history. Not that he minded that part, either. What he did mind was standing this close to her, so close he could feel the heat from their bodies mingling in the chilly air of the pantry when there was nothing he could do about it. They weren't twenty-year-olds who were just going to bang each other against the shelves of cereal and potatoes. She would want more than that. Hell, he was pretty sure he did, too.

"Isn't it great?" she pressed.

"It is." He cleared his throat and stepped backward into the kitchen before his imagination could run any further with that line of thinking. Pax knew he wanted her, and given the way they'd been together the other night, he thought there was a chance she might want him, too. But he'd wait. He'd bide his time. None of this was right. Even with as much desire as he held for her, she wasn't right for him. Pax had given up on finding his true mate, but even someone he settled down with had to at least be a shifter. "So, what do you have on the list for the kitchen?"

With a wry smile, Carrie flipped to the next page of the notebook. She turned it around and showed it to him.

In the same perfect script, she'd written 'Kitchen' at the top of the page. The rest of it was completely blank.

She swirled her hand through the air to indicate the entire room. "The whole thing is a giant task list.

The water and electricity work, but I imagine that's only because this place has been a rental house for so long. They have to give you utilities, but they don't have to make it pretty."

Pax could see what she meant. The plywood cabinets had been treated the same way that window in the dining room had, with so many layers of paint plastered onto them that it was probably what was holding them together after all these years. They were functional, but they were also incredibly plain compared to some of the other woodwork in the house. He reached out and rested his hand on one of the knobs—the years of corrosion not entirely pleasant in his hand—before he turned to her. "Do you mind?"

"Not at all."

Pax opened the cabinet to find exactly what he would've guessed was in there. Whole grain this and organic that. He pushed a couple of boxes aside, more interested in the construction of the cabinets than what was inside them. "Definitely not original to the house. Cabinets aren't cheap, though. This could be where you spend most of your money."

"And I think I'll be glad to if it also means I can get rid of these hideous countertops and old flooring." She frowned at the yellow laminate with chrome edging and the old linoleum.

"Someone probably remodeled back in the sixties," he guessed, having seen things like this plenty of times before. "It's a shame because what was in here before might have been beautiful. Everyone's always so eager to rip it all out and buy new, but that's not necessarily better." His eyes drifted back to hers, as they always did, and he thought he saw a ripple of something in those gemstone depths. Vulnerability? Hope?

Whatever it was, Carrie quickly buried it again. "If you think this is bad, you should see the upstairs." Without asking him if he even wanted to, she charged out the other door of the kitchen and up to the second floor. "Watch the handrail. I don't think it's all that sturdy."

Pax felt the wood shiver under his hand in agreeance. He followed her, and he would have regardless. This power she had over him was both unsettling and calming. Pax knew he wanted someone to be with. He wanted to come home at the end of the day, shower all the sawdust from his skin, and tell his partner how things had gone. He wanted to stand side-by-side with his partner as they cooked dinner, and he had to admit that he wanted to know he wasn't alone in his bed every night. He'd seen other members of his clan—some of whom he'd never imagined would turn away from a playboy lifestyle—suddenly turn into giant saps when they found the women they were supposed to be with.

But as he watched her curves sway up the stairs, Pax was once again chiding himself for wasting his time. This was a woman who wouldn't settle. She'd see right through him if she thought for a second that was what he was trying to do. She was experienced, but she was also a couples counselor. She'd diced him apart several times already and put him back together again. A woman like Carrie wouldn't be interested in a man like him, a man who'd thus far made himself a permanent bachelor.

"Okay, if you thought the rest was bad, check this out." Carrie reached the landing, and she crossed the hallway to a door. She opened it and stepped inside, waving her arm across the room as she presented it to him. "I give you the master suite."

"Oh." The influx of colors was almost too much to manage. The wallpaper had probably been put up around the same time as the kitchen, but in here, they'd gone for a more psychedelic vibe with big, swooping florals. The light fixture, a conglomeration of multicolored glass, shed a nauseating light over the shag carpeting. The one saving grace was that no one had gotten around to painting the woodwork, but that was about it. "Groovy."

Carrie laughed, a sound that shivered down into his bones and resonated through his body. "Pretty bad, right? And it goes great with my bedspread."

He hadn't even bothered to notice because it wasn't the hideous, glaring blemish that the rest of the room was. A soft down comforter of pure white lay over the mattress, crisply made even though she hadn't expected anyone to come over. The pillow shams and the blanket folded at the end of the bed were patterned in a pale blue toile. His mouth went completely dry. Pax shoved his hands in his pockets, keeping his arms at bay because they longed to pull her toward him and down onto the bed. To make love to her, yes, but more than that. To lay there with her, to feel her body against his.

Shit, what was happening to him?

Carrie laughed again, jarring him out of his fantasy. Reality wasn't exactly much better, since it still meant he was standing there with her at the foot of her bed. "I know it's bad, but you don't have to look so shocked," she said. "The other bedrooms up here aren't any better, which is why I went ahead and moved into this one. Terrible, right?"

"Pretty bad," he admitted, talking about himself just as much as the room.

"Well, that pretty much sums it up, so you can see what I've been doing with all my spare time." She tucked her notebook back under her arm and led the way out of the room and down the stairs. "It's going to be one hell of a project, and I have no idea when I'd be ready to open."

Pax focused on the house. That was what they'd been talking about, after all. She hadn't yanked him inside, pressed her lips against his, and tossed him down in front of the fireplace when he'd knocked on the door. That would've been perfectly fine with him, of course. "You could always do a room at a time and open your availability as the remodel goes along."

"I was thinking the same thing." She reached the bottom of the stairs and paused to look up at him as he came down behind her. Carrie's eyes were practically sparking with lightning now. "It's funny you stopped by tonight. I was actually going to call you."

Why did his heart skip a beat just then?

"I have a strange question to ask you," she continued. "Are you interested in fixing up the woodwork in here?"

Pax had never been the sort of man who talked

constantly, but Carrie had a way of chasing all the words out of his mouth. He gaped at her as he willed his brain and tongue to start functioning in unison again.

"I'd pay you, of course," she added quickly. "I don't know what your rates are, but you seemed interested in that aspect of this house from the moment you walked in two nights ago. I'm sorry, because I know this is such a strange thing to ask given how short our history is, but you seemed to know your stuff. And, I admit, when I started looking up remodelers and carpenters online today in between clients, your name came up quite a few times."

From the bottom of the stairs, he could see quite a bit of the main floor. There really was a lot of work to be done, and he'd originally planned on doing it all for himself, at his own pace, and most likely for his own profit. But as he looked into her eyes, none of it mattered anymore. "Yeah. That'd be great."

7
———

Carrie rolled over and nestled back down into the pillow. Her head was thumping and her mouth was dry. She was utterly miserable, but she was too exhausted to do anything about it.

The thumping came again, and now she realized it wasn't in her head at all. The sound was distant, like it was coming from somewhere else in the house, but it didn't seem to be stopping. Shit. Someone was at the door.

Sitting up was hard enough. Her head felt like it was full of concrete, so heavy, she thought she might fall into the pillow and not get back up again. A pair of sweats and a t-shirt lay over the back of her chair, and she yanked them on.

"The damn house better be on fire if someone's

pissing their pants so bad to get in," she grumbled to herself. Her head really was pounding, she realized as she navigated the stairs. She'd had far too much champagne the night before. How long had it been since she'd had that much to drink? Her stomach roiled, reminding her that she didn't want to know.

Clomping the last bit of the way to the front door, Carrie was ready to tell whoever it was that she wasn't interested in buying anything, nor was she going to convert to their religion. She sighed as she flicked back the lock and yanked open the door. Then she gasped, closing the door enough to hide the lovely ensemble she'd thrown on. Her crappy old bleach-stained sweatpants were the same ones she used to clean the bathtub in, and her t-shirt's graphic had crumbled away over the years, now looking like little more than dust across her braless chest.

It was Pax, looking to be in far better shape than she was. He held a toolbox in one hand and a tool bag in the other, smiling. The daylight behind him was far too bright. "Well, good morning, Sunshine. Did I wake you?"

"What are you doing here so early?"

He shook his head, looking both sympathetic and amused. "It's ten o'clock. That's when you told me to show up."

"Shit." Carrie rubbed her forehead. She remembered it all now. It wasn't as though she'd been so drunk that she'd blacked out. She'd asked him to help her with the house, and in her eagerness, she'd told him they'd start the very next day. "I'm sorry."

"I can come back another time if you'd like," he offered. "It wouldn't be until tomorrow night, though. I'll be logging during the day."

"No, no. Come in. I'm just not awake yet." She backed up to let him in, quickly crossing her arms across her chest.

Pax stepped inside and carefully put his tools down on the floor. "Where do you want to start? I thought a room-by-room approach might be the most efficient. Did you want to get one of the bedrooms started so it'll be ready for a guest?"

"Uh, how about the kitchen," she sputtered out, trying to think of someplace safer. She needed a decent kitchen if there was any chance of her feeding guests, anyway. "That's probably the worst room."

"Kitchen it is." He picked up his tools and led the way.

She was grateful to be looking at his backside instead of him looking at hers. He wore a gray t-shirt with a flannel thrown over it, but he removed it and took the liberty of setting it on the back of a kitchen chair. His arms were strong and muscled, honed from the work he did. She knew from his dating survey that he was a logger, and of course, there'd been plenty of discussion about his carpentry. Apparently, wielding a sander and moving all those logs around had been great for his physique. Carrie liked seeing the broad shoulders and rugged muscles that were earned and not simply the gift of youth.

His back was to her as he began measuring the length and width of the room. "You've got a couple of options when it comes to cabinets. There are some pretty affordable pre-mades down at the home improvement store. They cost less and they're quick, but you'll have the same kitchen as everyone else in town."

"Or?" She hadn't thought there would be an option besides that. Carrie had saved plenty of inspiration photos online, but she hadn't given much thought as to where the fixtures would come from. She leaned on the kitchen chair for support, and her hand came in touch with Pax's flannel, still warm from his body.

"Or I can make them." Pax ran the tape measure along the countertop. "It's slower and more expensive, but you'll get exactly what you want. Plus, we can make sure everything fits into the space perfectly without any weird gaps like this one." He used the tip of the tape measure to point at the dusty crevice between the stove and the wall.

"Wait, you can *make* them?" She pressed one hand against her head, feeling it still pound. Her heart was thudding along, which didn't do her headache any favors.

"Yep. Do it all the time. Like I said, it'll take a bit. In the meantime, I can fix the doors and drawers on this set in here so it's more functional. Probably need to replace the trim around this window, too. Do you know what style of cabinets you're looking for? I have some pictures of the ones I've done that I can show you." He put the tape measure down and approached her as he pulled his cell phone out of his pocket. Pax opened a gallery and flipped through gorgeous kitchens that looked too good to be true. "Something like this might be good, with clean lines, solid wood, and a few upper cabinets to give it a little more air and space."

"It's beautiful," she said, pointing over her shoulder in the vague direction of the stairs as she began backing up. "You know, I really need to run upstairs and get ready for the day. I'm running a little behind. You get started with anything you can, and I'll be back in a bit." As soon as she reached the doorway, she turned and scuttled for the stairs.

When her feet touched the horrid shag carpeting in her room, she shut her door and leaned against it. This was ridiculous. Why should she care how he saw her? He'd already seen her completely naked, so what was the difference if she wasn't wearing a bra or hadn't put on any mascara? That was just the sort of thing she cautioned her clients against. They had to love each other even when they were at their most unflattering.

Of course, this wasn't love. This was just some beefcake who suddenly seemed to be a part of her life, whether she meant for him to be or not. As she crossed into the bathroom, she scolded herself for being so shallow. She hardly knew the guy, aside from just how talented he was with his hands, yet here she was acting like it was going to turn into something.

Carrie turned on the water and began pulling off her clothes. She paused and shut the bathroom door, even though the bedroom door was already shut. Then she locked it. Pax wasn't the sort of guy who'd come barging in. Right? Right. But then her mind summoned an image of him coming up the stairs to ask her what sort of cabinet door handles she wanted, finding her soapy and naked in the shower, and then jumping in with her, those hands of his skimming through the lather over her body.

"Stop it," she whispered harshly to herself as she finished undressing and plunged into the water. Carrie looked down at her body. Being a woman in her forties was vastly different from being a man in his. A guy that age was still considered virile and attractive, distinguished even. A woman? Who'd grown two human beings in her belly? At the same time? Nothing was quite in the same place as it used to be. Her left knee ached when she sat in the same position too long, and she was a road trip buzzkill now that she had to pee all the time.

Angry with herself for being so hard on her own body, Carrie scrubbed at her hair. It was easier to analyze other people instead of herself, but right now, she wished she could step back and get a good look at what was going on in her life. She'd had a few flings since she'd become single. They were never anything that would lead to a long-term relationship, and she'd been able to enjoy herself even in knowing that. No man besides Brian had ever complained that her boobs weren't perky enough or that she had too much junk in her trunk, yet she'd chosen now to start worrying about such things.

It was time to stop.

Finishing her shower, Carrie stepped out and dried off. She unlocked the bathroom door and boldly whipped it open, finding her bedroom empty just as she thought she would. Dressing in a pair of jeans and a sweatshirt, she went back into the bathroom to put her makeup on. She paused as she leaned over the counter with her concealer stick in her hand. This was exactly what she'd been telling herself she didn't need to do. How Pax thought of her shouldn't make any difference. If he'd wanted more than the fling they'd already had, then he never would've agreed to come into her house and work for her.

Of course, she probably needed to run to the store later. And there was always a chance that a client could stop in. And didn't she deserve to look nice for herself, if not for anyone else? She compromised with a toned-down version of her usual look before she went back downstairs, summoning the reserved nature she'd built so carefully over all her years as a therapist.

8

The water had shut off upstairs. He could no longer hear it running through the pipes. Pax noted several more measurements in his phone, where they would be handy when he needed to work up the plans for the kitchen and while he was at the home improvement store buying materials. The numbers were automatic, and he'd put them all together later when he wasn't listening to every footstep of Carrie's upstairs.

It wasn't that he meant to, but he felt a certain sense of triumph. He'd thought she'd looked fine for a morning meant to be spent moving through the house, making decisions, and possibly even sweating if they got started on something. There wasn't any need for her to be dressed up if she was just going to look at cabinet doors and stain samples.

Unless there was.

He felt the corner of his mouth tweak upward as he grabbed a screwdriver from his bag and adjusted the hinge on a cabinet door that was hanging crookedly. These were shoddy old cabinets, but he wasn't about to tear them out until he had new ones ready. He'd get all the plans together and get started on the build in the evenings after he'd been logging. Sure, he had a couple of other projects to finish, but Pax liked to be busy. He liked knowing there was another undertaking to dive into as soon as he was through with the current one. That would leave the weekends for coming to Carrie's to work on floors, trim, and whatever else she needed.

He pulled out a drawer, frowned at the way the front was attached to the box, and adjusted it so it would close instead of bumping into the other drawer fronts above and below it. He could still hear Carrie above him. If she was trying to be quiet, the floor betrayed her with its squeaking. It was too easy to visualize what it would be like to live in a big house like this with a woman like her. Lazy Sunday mornings in bed, rolling over and making love, a slower, more sensual repeat of the night before.

Coffee in the dining room, or out on the porch in the warmer months. She would pull a book off the shelf and read, while he'd fix the toilet that kept running or went out to the garage to make a coat rack. Her gorgeous eyes flicking up to see him when he walked in the room, a small smile on her face that said she knew something about him that no one else did. Anyone else might look at Carrie and see the rigid exterior she put on when she was talking to a client. It wasn't cold, not really. It was just unattached, a little wall around herself. But he knew the way around it and into the softness of her embrace. After dinner, or when he just needed to blow off a little steam, it'd be easy to step out the back door and go for a quick run in his bear form.

Whoa. No.

Pax finished in the kitchen and moved into the dining room to take measurements and notes. He wasn't sure where Carrie would want to start while the cabinets were being made, but at least he could have his figures in order, no matter what she decided. In the meantime, *he* had to decide that he wasn't going to pursue this any further than what was required to do the work. He liked to fix and restore things, and she needed that done.

She was incredible, but she was human.

The living room was next as he made his rounds on the ground floor. At least he couldn't hear her upstairs, but it didn't make much of a difference when he looked at the fireplace. She might as well have been standing right there with him, running her fingers down the inside of his forearm as she whispered to him, reminding him of just how good it had felt.

He clenched his teeth down on his tongue as he felt his bear surge inside him once again. How could the damn thing want her so much when she was so wrong for them? What would she do if she ever found out? Just because there were a few humans that had mated with other clan members didn't make it the rule. It was the exception, and a rare one. A human woman would never understand that there was a side of him unlike anything she'd ever seen before.

And yet, they'd certainly understood each other a few nights ago. There had been no protests about how little they knew one another, that it wasn't right, or that they should slow down. Their bodies knew each other even if their minds didn't, speaking on a level that didn't require words.

"Pax."

His name on her lips rippled through his body.

He turned around to see her coming down the stairs in jeans, sneakers, and a sweatshirt. She wasn't dressed much differently than she'd been when he'd shown up. Her wet hair was pulled into a bun, a few loose curls snaking out just at the nape of her neck. Her eyes focused on the wooden stairs beneath her while her hand gripped the rail. She may as well have been making a grand entrance to a ball with the grace and confidence she had in her body, and he found himself moving closer, looking up and feeling his very blood swell toward her.

Her eyes flicked to him for only a moment. "Oh, good. There you are. Sorry it took me so long. I was just thinking about the cabinets. If they're going to be a bit, maybe we should start in one of the bedrooms. The one on the south end of the house would probably be the best candidate. I can show you what I'm thinking about doing, and—oh!" The flimsy handrail that she'd warned him about before gave way. The skinny balusters that had been used to hold it up weren't firmly attached to the stair treads.

Carrie must have been leaning into the railing more than it looked because she didn't fall straight down the stairs but off to the side, tumbling down after the pieces of broken wood. Pax's bear kicked his human body into high gear as he darted forward, catching her just before she fell onto the hardwood floor beneath her. She flailed for only a moment in his arms before she stilled, her chest heaving, her hands clutching at his t-shirt.

His blood thrummed through his body, and his senses took in every aspect of her. Waves of rose and vanilla washed over him, fresh and mingling with the soap and shampoo she'd used. She was still damp and warm beneath her clothing, tantalizing him into thinking what she must've looked like while she was in the shower.

"Are you all right?" he finally managed to ask, coming to his senses and slowly setting her on her feet.

"I—I think so." She kept her arms around his neck as she regained her balance and glared up at the offending hole in the railing. "It's a good thing you were here."

"Yeah. I guess that means we have another thing to add to the list." He felt cold as she let go of him, as though the parts of him that she'd touched were now thrown out into the February air.

She put a shaky smile on her face as she turned back to him. "What, you don't think my future guests will appreciate it? It's just part of my open floor plan."

It was a horrible joke, but he felt a chuckle rise inside him anyway. "We'll find a quick replacement for it. In the meantime, why don't I show you what I did in the kitchen, and then we can go from there. I'd better get back to it if I'm going to have time for my regular job on top of this."

As they moved back to the kitchen, even though she was never more than a few feet away from him, Pax distinctly felt her absence. If this house required as much work as he thought it did, then he'd be employed for at least several months. He hadn't decided if that was a good thing or a bad thing.

9

"It's driving me crazy, quite frankly."

"Paige!"

"Well, it's true," Paige insisted. "It's really hard for me to say, but I'm tired of keeping it inside all the time. Every time we need to go somewhere, you don't even bother peeling yourself up off the couch or getting your ass out of bed until the very last minute. Meanwhile, I've spent the whole morning trying to get everything ready."

Spencer threw his hands in the air and let them flop back down to his lap. "That's because you've already kept me up half the night worrying about how many pairs of socks to bring. It's not my fault you have to batten down the hatches and pack everything but the kitchen sink just to go to the grocery store."

"I'm not talking about the damn grocery store!"

"Folks." Carrie spoke quietly and lifted her hand just above the notebook she was using. "It's good to get these things out, but let's think about our tone of voice and the words we're using. You can be truthful without being hurtful. Talk to your partner the way you expect your partner to talk to you. Let's try it again."

Paige let out a huff that made the strand of hair hanging near her face float up in the air. "It really bothers me that you don't help when we go somewhere."

Impatience was still written all over Spencer's face, but he gave it a shot as well. "It really bothers me that you stress so much about it. I mean, if we forgot something at home, we can usually buy it somewhere along the way."

"Good." Carrie nodded, encouraging her new clients. These were some of the first locals who'd come to her since she'd moved to Carlton. She could see that they had a few issues to work out, but it wasn't anything she hadn't encountered before. There was nothing more important than making them feel as though she'd done her job, both because she took pride in her work and because they very well might tell their friends and help her establish her new clientele.

Of course, it was a little harder to concentrate when she was so aware of Pax in the next room. He'd come by when he was done with logging for the day, smelling of earth, pine, and sawdust, and asked if he should get started on a few other projects while he waited for her to decide on the kitchen cabinets. Now she could hear him through the closed door of her office, scraping the years of paint off the window in the dining room. Her office back in Sacramento had been in a suite among many other professionals, and even when the doors were closed, she could hear phones ringing or the muffled sounds of conversations. Carrie had been able to tune that out, but Pax was completely different.

She clenched her hand around her pen, forcing herself to focus. "Now, help me understand a little more about this particular situation. What kind of places are you talking about going to? Is this a trip to the grocery store, or is it a vacation?"

"His family lives two hours away," Paige explained, looking exhausted. "We visit at least once a month, which means it's an entire day by the time we drive up there, visit, and drive home. I've got to make sure our pets are taken care of and our kids are all packed up, and by the time I do all that, I don't even have time to get myself ready."

Spencer shrugged his shoulders. "I've been living far away from my family for a long time. Heck, I used to drive four hours from the base just to come home for a bit on the weekends when I was still in the service. I'm just used to it. And really, if we forget to bring the baby wipes or something, we can just buy some."

"Sure," his wife agreed, "but that's never just a simple trip down to the corner store. The last time we did that, we spent over a hundred dollars."

Carrie could see that this was about much more than just the trips themselves. "You often find two different kinds of people together in a relationship. We've all heard the old trope about spenders versus savers, but it can be other things, too. A night owl and a morning person. A homebody and a world traveler. We often fall in love despite our differences, and I think that's what you've got going on here. Paige, you like to be prepared and make sure everything is taken care of. Spencer, you'd rather worry about a problem the moment it arises instead of getting concerned about it ahead of time."

They both bobbed their heads enthusiastically,

clearly happy to see that someone understood where they were coming from.

That vindication, hopefully, would help them give a little to each other. "The thing is, you can't change who someone naturally is inside. You can ask a messy person to pick their socks up off the floor, but you probably won't turn them into a neat freak. The solution isn't to force one to be like the other. It's to find a way to accept each other for who you are in a way that works for both of you."

Paige was leaning forward now, interested. "So, what do we do?"

Carrie rolled her hand in the air. "That's what I want the two of you to figure out together. I'm not saying I won't help, of course, but only the two of you will know what works best for your daily lives. And I don't want you to think up something you want your partner to do to make you feel better about the situation. I want you to think of what *you* can do to make your partner feel better."

Paige's mouth went a little slack, and Spencer's brows shot up. They'd never thought about it like that before, but in Carrie's experience, most people hadn't. Couples were always focused on changing each other, not themselves.

"Um, what if we put an emergency duffel bag in

the back of the van with some essentials? It would just stay there all the time, so we'd always have some backup diapers and wipes and things," Spencer suggested.

She nodded, starting to look a little less stressed. "And I could be a bit more flexible when it comes to how much we have to take with us. Things don't have to be perfect."

"There you go. That's a great start. You've got a physical thing you can easily achieve, so don't lose sight of that. Pack that emergency bag—together—as soon as you get home. That way, it doesn't get brushed off or forgotten. I think you'll both feel a lot better about that. We don't always have control over things, including our partners. This is a great step toward accepting and understanding each other. When is your next trip to see your family?"

"This coming weekend, actually," Spencer admitted. "That's why it's a bit of a hot-button issue right now."

"Perfect. Then you guys can tell me how it went when you come in next week." Their time was up, and Carrie walked with them to the door. She'd taken Jenna's advice to start utilizing the driveway that wrapped around the side of the house and right to the office. It would keep her therapy clients separate from the future bed and breakfast guests, plus it simply felt more professional not to march everyone through her home.

She shut the door behind them, but the long glass pane allowed her to see the couple as they walked out to their minivan. His fingers brushed against hers, and her eyes were soft when she looked up at him. They would probably still have several arguments over those long family visits, but they were trying. The effort was the most important thing.

Carrie was still smiling to herself when she headed out of her office and into the dining room, her empty coffee cup in hand. She jolted and nearly dropped her mug when she saw Pax standing there. She'd allowed herself to get distracted enough by Spencer and Paige that she'd actually forgotten about him for a few minutes, which had been a nice respite.

He bent to put the scraper in his toolbox, and those deep midnight eyes were curious when he lifted them to her. "You got a second?"

"Sure." Carrie wrapped her hands around her mug, wishing it was still warm. The cold ceramic was little diversion when faced with Pax. He'd only just started doing this work around the house for her, but she had to wonder if she'd ever get used to him being there.

He noted her coffee cup and jerked his head toward the kitchen. "I'll follow you."

"You want some? Coffee?" she added quickly.

"That'd be nice."

"The cream and sugar are right there if you need it. What did you want to talk to me about?" She grabbed another mug out of the cabinet and poured the hot, black liquid inside before handing it to him. His fingers grazed hers as he took it, and a frisson of energy jolted up her arm and through her body.

"The house, of course." He took a sip of the coffee, not seeming to mind that it was hot as lava. "I know we mostly just talked about the woodwork that needed to be done, but I have some other skill sets that might come in handy."

Damn right he does. Carrie frowned at the cup of coffee she poured for herself, trying not to let her mind wander off into the gutter. "Such as?"

"You mentioned taking down the wallpaper in the dining room and painting. It would make sense to do that before I refinish the china cabinet or the floor, just in case there are any drips. It also means we don't have to go back and do any of it later.

We. He threw that term around easily enough,

and Carrie had to wonder exactly what he meant by it. Neither of them had said a word about their tryst. In fact, Pax talked about the house so much that she was starting to think he'd only hooked up with her to get a better look at the hardwood floor in front of the fireplace. Now she was being ridiculous again. He'd said he would do the work on the house, and it was about to be her house, so it only made sense that there was some sort of 'we' involved in that. "I suppose you're right. Do you have time for all that, though? You mentioned you have a lot of other work."

"I do, but..." He trailed off and lifted a shoulder, dismissing his other concerns and choosing not to explain how he was going to fit it all in. "I like to know that things are done right."

She leaned against the counter near the coffee pot. A thrill moved through her at knowing Pax would be there even more often than he was now, and probably for a longer time period overall. "If it means getting the place ready for guests a little quicker, then I don't see how I can turn that down. Are you as good with paint as you are with wood?"

"If the people on those home improvement shows can do it, so can I. I painted my whole place, actually. I can show you if you'd like proof." He reached for the pocket where she now knew he kept his cell.

"That's all right. I believe you." Carrie quickly waved away the notion. She didn't need him to come stand next to her like that again, to have his arm against hers and his cheek close as they both tried to look at a small screen together. In fact, she needed to do a much better job of keeping her distance from him. Pax hadn't said a single word about the two of them getting together for anything other than what the house required. She thought she might've caught a glance here or there, but nothing that told her he was interested in pursuing what he'd started. That was fine. It just meant she needed to let go of her physical attraction for him. Surely, she could do that. She'd coached couples who'd had affairs and helped them turn their affection back to each other. Why should it be so hard to train her own interests?

"Do you have a color picked out? I can grab it sometime this week."

"I do, actually. I've got the swatch in my office." Carrie led the way to the back of the house. She sat in her desk chair as she retrieved the card out of her drawer, one that showed a shade of warm, buttery yellow. "I thought it'd go nicely with the darker wood."

"Works for me." He barely gave it a glance before he put it in his pocket and turned to go back into the dining room. He paused in the doorway. "Did you really mean all that?"

"All of what?" She looked up at him, realizing that most of the times when she'd spoken to him thus far, they were always both standing. The dynamic was different now that she was sitting down. It was all part of body language and human interactions, things she'd studied in detail. Carrie knew how people used just this sort of thing when they wanted to make someone feel a certain way. She had a good notion that Pax wasn't doing any of it on purpose, but it made her feel vulnerable. The biggest problem with that was she wasn't sure if she loved it or hated it.

Coffee mug still in one hand, he swept the other one toward the couch where her clients sat. "All that stuff about couples accepting each other for who they really are."

"You were eavesdropping?" Anger rippled through her chest. "Pax, that's not okay. Folks come here expecting completely private sessions."

"Relax. It wasn't anything I was doing on purpose. The walls are just a bit thin here. It makes me think you might not have enough insulation, which is something else we'll need to address at some point."

"Oh." She put her defenses back down. She hadn't wanted to be angry with him in the first place. Carrie hadn't judged him to be the sort of man who listened in on private meetings, and it was good to know she was right. "I did mean that, actually. I think acceptance is one of the biggest things that can keep a marriage together. I focused on it a lot in my book. Two people can learn to live with each other in many ways, but fixing a few habits or talking things out can only go so far if you don't surrender yourself to the notion that your partner is a completely different entity from yourself."

"I see." He still lingered in the doorway, hesitant.

"Why do you ask?" Carrie wondered if the overheard conversation had simply piqued his curiosity or if there was some genuine reason he'd wanted to know. Everyone wanted a little free therapy if they could get it.

Pax tipped his head to the side, pulling in a breath and holding it for a minute. "It's just hard for me to believe that someone who genuinely feels that way could be divorced."

The nerve he struck sent a vibration of annoyance running through her as though he'd rung a bell. Her failed relationship had nearly made her change her career entirely. Carrie's heart squeezed as her mind rushed back to those dark days when she'd sat on her bed, crying into her pillow and wondering why she'd ever fooled herself into thinking she could help others when she couldn't even help herself.

She'd come a long way since then. In fact, the question wouldn't have bothered her at all if it hadn't come from Pax. She knew that was true because she'd fielded it before with ease. Carrie tapped into those same answers because she knew they were still just as true as they'd been the other times she'd given them. "I firmly believe that both partners have to feel that way. There's not much point, otherwise."

His face changed a little. Satisfied, maybe? Pleased? Pax had made himself more challenging to read than most people. He could be hard and stubborn, but Carrie distinctly sensed some softness and understanding as well.

"Makes sense. I'd better get back to this." He lifted his cup of coffee in a small salute before he left, shutting the office door behind him and leaving her alone.

Even when she could once again hear the steady scraping on the dining room window, Carrie sat at her computer and stared at the screen. What was it that someone hadn't accepted in Pax? The long hours he enjoyed working with his hands? She smiled as she had further proof of what she'd always known about relationships: It was all relative. One person might be thrilled to have a man who was always busy fixing things because they appreciated his contribution to the household. Another would be frustrated by all the time he spent away from her in his woodshop or wherever. One's flaws could be attributes just like trash to treasure. It was an intriguing concept, one that she wanted to make sure she worked into either a workshop session or potentially a future book. Carrie grabbed her fountain pen and jotted down some notes.

10

Rain had drizzled down the windows all night long, but it'd been reduced to a heavy cloud cover this morning. Pax moved through the thick forest, looking for the next tree. He could hear the distant sound of Dean on the other side of the hill, downing one. The scent of tree sap and earth was thick in the damp air. It was the sort of day that usually put Pax in a good mood. It made him feel like it was the only place in the world where he belonged, and he was grateful he had a job that paid him to be out there.

But as he selected a large pine with a straight trunk, he knew he wasn't. His bear was usually satisfied to be out in the woods, even when Pax was in his human form. It was a connection to nature that many people didn't get in their day-to-day lives, yet the only place he wanted to be was at Carrie's.

Glancing up and around to check that there would be a clear path for the tree to fall, Pax felt his dissatisfaction deepen. He'd been able to let go of Carrie buying the house out from under him. Hell, he hadn't even bothered to tell her he'd been the person she'd outbid. The idea had entertained him for a moment, but in the end, he'd decided to leave it alone. The last thing he wanted was to give her any reason to apologize to him.

He fired up the chainsaw and hefted it to begin the notch that would control the direction of the fall. Damp sawdust spewed out of the fresh wound. Already, Carrie had shown him more and more of the side of herself that others didn't see. That same hard veneer he'd spotted on her the first night returned whenever she met with clients. She studied, helped, and encouraged them to bring out their innermost secrets, yet she never gave that secret soft part of herself over to them. Pax only got a glimpse of her in action here and there as he worked on the house, but he knew what was happening.

She even kept a bit of that wall up when she spoke to him, either in the kitchen over coffee or as they were discussing which shade of stain looked best, but it crumbled swiftly, leaving mere remnants behind. What might happen if he actually put her in a position of apologizing? What if there was nothing but the delicate sweetness of her? How could he possibly ignore that? How could he do anything but pull her into his arms and show her just how difficult it'd been to keep his distance from her over the past week?

With the top angled cut of the notch made, Pax started in on the lower cut that would remove a large wedge of wood from the trunk. The tree would fall in this direction, right onto the old farming road. A branch or two might break loose from the other trees around it, but it would be a clean cut with no damage.

If only relationships were that easy. Make a decision, cut in, and then stand back to observe your work. It was a wonder that Carrie bothered to deal in anything as messy as marriage, divorce, and love.

As he moved to the far side of the tree and checked his angles before making the final cut, he remembered how he'd spent the last part of the night. It was late, and he should've been in bed if he was going to get up early and start logging. But since he'd been unable to get Carrie off his mind, he'd instead found the goodie bag that she'd given him at the speed dating event. Somehow he'd still had it shoved in his jacket pocket. The chocolate was darker than he preferred, but he found the coupon code for her book.

Building, Bonding, Better was definitely not the sort of book Pax ever would've picked up on his own, coupon or not. But when he'd downloaded the ebook version last night, it had nothing to do with how he felt about relationships. It had been about Carrie. Though it was part of her professional life, and that was a side of her that he knew wasn't quite the same as the warm, sexy woman who'd gasped in his arms, he still felt that it would tell him something about her. It was obvious already that she cared about her career as a therapist; otherwise, she would've abandoned it completely to follow this bed and breakfast dream.

What he found in the few chapters he read reflected exactly what he'd heard her talk about when it came to her sessions. It was about acceptance, grace, understanding, and communication. Carrie had written extensively about various couples she'd met and what she'd helped them to do to see how the other person felt. She discussed at length that a person had to not only accept their spouse's flaws, but their own as well.

The tree shivered a little, letting him know that he'd gone just the right depth into the trunk. He pulled out the chainsaw, cut the engine, and moved away. It didn't matter that he'd done this thousands of times. It didn't matter that he'd been a part of the logging operation his entire life, and so had the man who'd trained him. The tree should simply fall as he'd directed it to with his cuts, but he never stuck around to prove that it wouldn't kick back and take him out at the knees or wobble a little on its stump before deciding to take its revenge on the person who'd cut it down.

He reached the top of the hill and turned just in time to see the tree fall, exactly as he'd predicted it would. Was that the same sort of precaution that Carrie was taking in her own life? She'd helped countless couples find happiness, but that didn't guarantee that she'd find any for herself. That could be why her eyes constantly shifted away from his when they spoke, and why she usually closed herself in her office when he was there, even if it was past her regular work hours.

This was the last tree of the morning, and when he finished topping it, he headed back to the skidder, now repaired of its faulty hose. He'd allowed all of that talk about acceptance to give him some faint hope that he could actually make things work between himself and Carrie. His inner bear was a part of him that he couldn't change. He wouldn't want to even if he could. But she was the sort of person who would stand back, look at the situation logically, and understand that it was just part of who he was.

No. She wrote about things like spending habits and time schedules and lifestyle, not whether someone could turn into another creature at will. Pax was glad he hadn't shared any of these thoughts with anyone. He'd feel like even more of an idiot than he did right now.

He'd still felt like an ass for making that comment about how she shouldn't be divorced if she was so perceptive and reasonable.

"Got everything dropped on the west side," he announced when he reached the others. "Might be a couple more I can drop once we get the downed ones skidded out of there and there's a little more room. How's the rest of it looking?"

James lifted his chin toward the timber truck with its flatbed trailer and upright posts. "Pretty good. Just need to finish securing this load so we can send it out."

"On it." Pax eagerly dove into the work. He was convinced that at some point, he'd be able to put Carrie behind him. She was just someone else that he worked for. He'd created customized, commissioned furniture for all sorts of people in Carlton. Some of them had been attractive women, but he'd never gone out of his way to flirt with them, spend time with them, or think about them. Carrie didn't have to be any different. He just had to control himself. If the people she talked about in her book could learn to get past all the difficulties and arguments they had with their spouses, then he sure as hell could put whatever feelings he had for her aside and go on living his life like he always had.

That was part of the problem, though. Pax didn't want to live his life like he always had. He'd already decided to find himself a mate of some sort. Being single was fine before, but now that he'd convinced himself he wanted something more, it was hard to settle for anything else. He'd have to find some time to get out, maybe stop in at The Warehouse or some of the bars downtown. Of course, that was going to be difficult if he was spending all his free time at Carrie's place.

Dean came up from the east side of the hill they'd been working, a sheen of sweat on his brow despite the cool day. He paused next to the truck. "Looks like you got it all loaded up."

"No thanks to you," Pax joked.

Evan, who'd just shut down the loader so he could get back on the skidder, shook his head. "You guys are ridiculously competitive."

"Don't discourage them," James warned. He carried a clipboard in one hand as he looked over their progress for the day. Most companies had switched over to tablets and apps, but James Thompson was more old-fashioned than that. Anytime someone brought it up to him, he always complained about how little cell service they got while working in such rural areas. No one could argue with that. "That ruthless drive is yet another reason we keep getting all these contracts."

"Still gloating over the Copeland project?" Pax asked with a grin, knowing his uncle was just as driven and competitive as the rest of them were.

"That, and there's another one that I've got to go look at later this afternoon," James replied. He flipped the sheet on his clipboard to find the information. "It turns out the Copelands have some friends by the name of Foster who are interested in making a little cash from the timber on their property. And, just like the Copelands, they don't want to see it all torn to pieces in the process. As soon as they heard about the way we do things, they gave me a call."

A metallic sound split through the air. Pax turned just in time to see the load of wood go tumbling to the ground. The massive logs, ones that had only been lifted onto the truck in the first place thanks to the modern miracle of hydraulics, came rolling down. Dean leaped out of the way, diving around behind James's truck just as his chainsaw was smashed into pieces. The earth shook with the vibrations.

"Holy shit!" Dean had his hands on his knees, and he looked pale.

Everyone else had jumped into action as well, but the only thing that could be done in the moment was to get the hell out of the way. The remaining load showed no sign of going anywhere, so now it was time to assess the damage.

James gripped his clipboard so hard his knuckles were white. "Dean, are you all right?"

"Am I all right? Fuck!" He puffed out some air and gasped for more. "I don't think I've had a close call like that in years. And never from the goddamn truck. What happened?"

His uncle looked like he was about to explode.

"The load wasn't secured. Pax, where was your head? I know it's been in the dang clouds all week, but we can't have this. You'll have to stop doing all your little side jobs if you're not getting enough sleep or something."

All the blood drained from Pax's face as he took in the massive log that lay on the cold ground and the chainsaw beneath it. If Dean hadn't been as quick on his feet, then those bits of smashed plastic could very well have been him. Pax slowly shook his head. "I know I've been busy, but I'd never let something like this happen."

"Hmph."

Pax turned around. He saw the way they looked at him. Damn. They'd all noticed that he hadn't quite been present. Pax thought he'd hid it better than that, but clearly, he'd been wrong. The thing was, he trusted himself more than that. Even if he was purely on autopilot, it was hard to imagine he could ever make such a big mistake with such dire consequences. Every part of his body shuddered with the thought that he might've killed a member of his clan. "That can't be right."

"Son, don't make me put you on leave," James warned. "I can't afford to lose one of my best men when we've got a shit ton of good contracts lined up like this."

The fact that he referred to Pax as 'son' only proved just how rattled James truly was. He rarely used any term of endearment unless there was something major happening, and all of the younger generation who worked for him were his sons as far as he was concerned.

The word only made Pax feel worse about what had happened. He skirted the fallen log that'd taken out the chainsaw. Two others had rolled off behind it, but they'd hit the ground without consequence. Pax's instincts told him there was something more going on. He pulled himself up onto the side of the flatbed, poignantly aware of just how much these logs weighed and how much damage they could inflict. It was part of their job, yes, but even at his most complacent, he never forgot just how risky it was. Every tool they used and every tree they felled could be considered deadly.

It didn't take him long to find the problem. His shoulders sagged with relief, but fury burned through his veins. "It wasn't me."

"What do you mean?"

Pax hopped down from the vehicle. He picked up one of the metal uprights that normally rose from the truck bed, then retrieved the bolt that was supposed to be holding it on. He'd spotted it from above, and it made his suspicions kick in. Picking up the bolt and examining it up close told him that he'd been right. "Check it out. This bolt sheared, but it had already been partially cut."

James swallowed as he took the offending fastener from his nephew. "Sure as shit. Look at that. You can tell where it was nipped here, and then where it ripped apart on this side once the full weight of the timber rested against it. It wouldn't have sheared off like that until the truck was full."

"I'm not sure if that makes me feel any better," Dean noted, looking angry now instead of scared.

Pax could still taste the adrenaline in his mouth, and he wasn't even the one who'd nearly been busted open like a watermelon. "This was bad enough, but I hate to think what would've happened if the load had held until it got on the highway."

The pale lines around James' mouth suggested he was thinking the same thing. "I hate to think what this implies."

"The Ballards?" Dean was now leaning on the bed rail of the truck. A bit of color had come back into his face, but he was clearly still getting over his close call. No one would blame him, not in the least.

He logged during the day and volunteered with the fire department in his spare time, so he was used to putting himself at risk.

"Most likely," James agreed. "Neither the Copelands nor the Fosters said anything about them putting a bid in on their land, but I didn't ask. It just wouldn't seem right to, but now I wish I had."

"You'd have no reason to," Pax countered, jiggling the bolt in his hand. He put it in his pocket, deciding it was better to keep the evidence. "They hadn't given us any trouble in quite some time. They've been working their properties, and we've been working ours."

"But if I heard right when I was talking to a few buddies of mine, the Ballards haven't been getting any good contracts lately," his uncle argued. "They could, if they wanted to do things nice and clean like we do. Hell, that's what they *ought* to be doing anyway if they give a shit about still having some places to come out and go for a run here and there. But they just want it fast and easy, and I'd gamble they're starting to see that's just not how it's done anymore."

"So let's take that bolt to the Ballards and tell them just what the fuck they can do with it." Not only had more color returned to Dean's face, but it was starting to redden with rage now that he knew exactly who was responsible. "If they want to play around, so can we."

"Hold on." James put a hand in the air. He no doubt sensed, just as Pax did, that this was about to turn into an ugly situation if he didn't reel it in a bit. "Even though I think it's very likely, we don't know for certain that the Ballards are responsible. In fact, I'd say we have very little proof that any of the things we've been experiencing over the last couple of weeks are even foul play. I don't want anyone going off half-cocked and making things worse. I'll bring the subject up to Chris to see what he wants to do about it."

Dean swiped a hand through his hair. To Pax, he didn't look like he was going to be able to contain himself very well. But he nodded. "Fine, I guess."

"I do understand how you feel," James said, patting his hand on Dean's shoulder. "Your life was already put at risk with this incident, and I don't want anything further to happen until we've got proof. Like I said, I'll take this up with Chris. In the meantime, we've got to be extra vigilant. Check every chain and brake line and piece of safety equipment, even if it's something you're familiar with. And we'll need to keep our eyes peeled for any signs that someone's been on our property or our contracted property without permission."

"That's going to be hard to do on our own." Evan put his foot up on the tailgate. "Shit, even if we put up cameras, we won't be able to cover everything."

James nodded his agreement. "I know. Just sit tight, okay? Do your jobs, and don't do anything that will let the Ballards know how much they've already gotten to us. Don't say a word about it because it'll only encourage them if they think they've already put us in a bind. Now let's get back to work. We've got to get the truck fixed so we can reload these logs. And Dean?"

"Yeah?"

"I guess you get to buy yourself a new chainsaw."

Pax went back to work. He was still distracted, but this time, it was by something other than Carrie. Would the Ballards really go to such lengths over a few contracts? He liked to think not, but in his heart, he knew better.

11

"It's very nice to meet you, Emery. Please have a seat." Carrie shook her new client's hand and gestured toward the comfortable couch.

He was a tall, broad man with a square jaw, built like many of the other men Carrie had seen around Carlton so far. Not unlike Pax in some ways. She had to wonder if it had something to do with so many of them being in the logging industry. That led her mind on a meandering path, curious about the Oregon Trail and if the pioneers who'd been tough enough to make it that far had produced generation after generation of rugged people. The only thing somewhat soft about him were his eyes, a pale shade of blue that looked around the room with interest.

"Thank you. I appreciate you seeing me. I know it's probably a little weird for a person to come in on their own." He sat on the edge of the sofa and ran a hand through his curly hair, scooting back a little further, trying to get comfortable.

Carrie smiled. So many times, whether in Carlton or Sacramento, she saw people who would barely touch their backside to the couch at the beginning of the session. By the end of the hour, they were practically sprawled out on it as they unloaded their life stories and past traumas and tried to figure out how it all related to their current lives. Just having someone to talk to could make a huge difference. "It happens more often than you think. Why don't you tell me a little about what made you decide to see me?"

She had to wonder herself. Carrie had started this session just like any other, but Pax's words were lurking in the back of her mind now. In the moment, she'd managed to put aside the anger and insult she'd felt when he'd questioned her advice on relationships when she didn't have one herself. It wasn't any of his damn business what she did with her relationships *or* what she said to her clients, especially since he wasn't involved in either one of those! But the simple question had been nagging at her for the last few days, making her wonder if she was qualified to have this job at all.

Emery braced his elbows on his knees and pressed his hands together. "I just wanted to come get a feel for how things are. You see, I'd like my fiancée to come with me. As soon as I told her, though, she kind of freaked out. She said people only went to marriage counseling when something was wrong."

"I see. Many people feel that way. They think of what happens here as a last resort, something you only do when you're on the brink of divorce. While that is the case sometimes, there are also many couples who come in to deepen their bond or to work on the smaller issues they may have before they become bigger ones." Her mind flashed back to the meager attempt at counseling that she and Brian had made before they split up. It'd been at her insistence because she knew it was the right thing to do. Of course, he hadn't liked the idea, and it hadn't helped. It hadn't kept them from signing the papers, nor had it stopped the cardboard boxes from stacking up in the living room or the other side of the bed suddenly being empty. Carrie still regretted those days, but not because she missed Brian. It was simply painful, and she knew Cat and Cam had suffered for it, too.

"Good," Emery replied with a bob of his head. "That's what I was telling her. I know there are some religions that make you do a form of counseling before you get married, so I was looking at this in a similar way. I just want to make sure we're both on the same page and that we set ourselves up for the best future together."

It was hard not to smile at him for that. Carrie didn't want to be sexist, but in her experience, it was usually the women who were most concerned about keeping the relationship going long-term. "While I can't say it's for everyone, I do think it helps. Many times, we let our love for each other cloud what's going on in our lives. We might look over someone's less appealing qualities simply because we don't want to lose the charm of being in love and in the middle of something new." She'd probably done plenty of that when she and Brian had first gotten together, and so had he. In those first few months and even years of their romance, it hadn't mattered that she preferred to read and study and that he wanted to go barhopping and play with his band.

They loved each other, and in those golden times, they'd thought they could make anything work.

"I don't know if we have any real issues, but I guess that's why I'm here. I want to see if we do. I figured if I came to meet with you first, I'd have some things I could take back to her. Eventually, I might be able to get her to come in with me."

Carrie nodded. "It's a nice idea, and it's considerate of you to come scout it out ahead of time so she knows what she'll be going into. Every session is slightly different, and that variance also depends on who is here and what they contribute. That means that even though you and I can certainly discuss your relationship, it won't be the same as if she were here. What's her name?"

He hesitated for a fraction of a second. "Jessica."

"Why don't you tell me a little about your relationship with Jessica." She sat back, relaxing more and hoping he would do the same. Her mind immediately drifted back to Pax. He wasn't there that day. He was out logging or doing whatever the hell else he wanted to do. It was none of her business, just as her practice wasn't his. Did he think all this advice she dished out to people was bullshit? That she just said things to make people feel better long enough to pay her?

Only her notetaking was keeping her from losing track of the conversation entirely. "Let's focus a bit more on what you just said about your family. Jessica is concerned you spend too much time with them?"

"Yeah. We're...close." He rolled a shoulder. "It's just how things have always been."

"And what about her family? What kind of dynamic do they have?"

"They're close, too. This past Christmas and Thanksgiving were our first big holidays together, and we were already getting into fights about whose family we would see on which day."

She scribbled a quick note, enjoying the deep purple ink she'd put in her pen that day. "That's a common situation for people. Sometimes it helps to work out a schedule in advance, odd years at this house and even years at another. It takes the decision off your shoulders because you just check the schedule and go with it. Do you think that might work for the two of you?"

Not that any of her suggestions meant anything. If they did, she might've made her own marriage work. Could a schedule keep two people together? Or anything else they'd agreed on? Damn it! She didn't even *want* to be with Brian anymore. He could come knocking on her door right now, and she'd send him packing. It was just that Pax had made her imposter syndrome rear its ugly head. Who was she to give advice to people?

"Someone said you wrote a book," Emery mentioned.

"I did." As she launched into her typical spiel about it and how the accompanying workbook would be coming out soon, Carrie straightened her shoulders. That was right. She'd written a book. Even more important than that was how her agent and publisher had eaten it up, asking for more as soon as they'd gotten through the first draft. It had shot up the bestseller list in no time, and Carrie had received a flood of emails, reviews, and social media comments praising her for it. All of that had to mean something. Right?

"We might check that out," Emery said, his eyes roving around the office again.

Carrie was used to that, and she'd created her office with just that sort of thing in mind. She never kept photos of her children in the office, especially when they were younger. When they were still together, she didn't even have a photo of herself and Brian displayed. It'd felt like she'd be rubbing her own marriage in the faces of those who'd come to her for help, even though her marriage had often been a rocky one. The plain gold band she'd worn in those times had been enough.

Now, with a whole new office to decorate just for herself, she'd done her best to create a space that was both comfortable and bright. The walls were painted a shade of champagne orange that she'd fallen in love with, and they were covered in various prints of flowers and countrysides. The furniture was comfortable and deep, but she'd chosen to move away from the dark leather that was so often associated with therapy and psychologists and more toward pastels and feminine elegance. With the long windows that graced one side of the room and let in an abundance of sunshine, it was one of her favorite places to be in the house.

"Are there any other issues you'd like to chat about?" she asked, leaning forward just to make herself focus. Pax had burst into her life unexpectedly, and now even when he wasn't there, it was impossible to ignore him. Maybe it wouldn't be so difficult if he hadn't said anything about her session and questioned her on the advice she gave. Could it be innocent? Well, maybe. She wouldn't have been so shocked by those words if they'd come from a client, but of course, the vast number of clients she'd built up in Sacramento certainly seemed to think she knew what the hell she was doing.

"I think that's really about it for now. I'll talk to her and see if I can get her to come in. Would it be all right if she didn't? I mean, if I needed to come back by myself?"

He was a brawny man, the kind who probably wouldn't ask for directions or call a tow truck. Yet there he was, being completely vulnerable in asking for her help and guidance. It was sweet, and she secretly wished he and his fiancée the best of luck in the future. If she had the same kind of consideration for him, the two of them were going to be just fine. "Of course, you can. Just give me a call. I don't always answer since I don't have an assistant. You can also use my website to book a session." She handed him a card from her desk that had all the information.

Emery took one last glance around the room as though he were trying to memorize it, perhaps so he could take all the details back to Jessica. "That sounds good. Thanks again for your time."

"Not a problem at all." She stood to walk him out as she usually did, but when his truck left the driveway, she turned and slumped against the door.

Emery had seemed happy enough with the session, but as far as she was concerned, it was an unmitigated disaster. Carrie checked her notes. The page was filled with lovely purple ink, and maybe if someone in another profession looked it over, they'd think her client had her full attention, but she knew it wasn't true. There would be so much there if she were actually on the ball.

Slapping the notes back down on the desk, she cursed Pax under her breath. It was all his fault. She'd worked through her doubts about moving her practice to Carlton, and thanks to all of Jenna's excellent marketing help, she knew she was going to make it just fine.

Until he had to open his mouth and say exactly what he thought.

The knock on the front door jolted her out of her reverie, and Carrie was glad no one else was in the office to see her jump. She carefully placed her fountain pen in its holder so it wouldn't roll off the desk and bend the nib. Checking the clock, she knew exactly who it had to be. It was as though she'd summoned him with all her angry thoughts about their conversation.

He was there on the porch with his tool bag in his hand like he always was, looking so eager, handsome, and downright delicious. Damn him again, why did she react to him like that? She was a grown woman and a professional, and it shouldn't matter that the corners of his eyes crinkled so pleasantly when he smiled.

His smile disappeared quickly. "Are you all right? You look mad."

She shook her head and took a moment to sort out her face while she held the door open for him. "I'm fine. I just...have a lot on my mind."

"I might have the perfect solution for you."

His voice rumbled into her ears and through her chest, reawakening that part of her that he'd brought to life so easily on the first evening they'd met. Carrie looked up, completely unsure of what her face said now. "You do?"

"Sure. We've got to get that handrail taken care of. I've been thinking about it quite a bit. Even if you're not ready for guests, it's not safe for you to have your stairs like that." He crossed through the entryway to the bottom of the stairs, frowning at the gaping hole she'd fallen through.

"Oh. Right." Definitely not at all where her mind had gone, but he was right. "I looked at some of the samples you showed me, and I looked online for some ideas, but I'm not sure."

"Good, because I have a completely different idea. What if we get something from the woods? A nice curved piece, naturally grown that way, would go beautifully here. We could still anchor it in a square newel post so it wouldn't take away from the craftsman style that the house was originally. I think it could make a great accent piece." He swept his hands along the empty space where the railing had once been, looking so enthusiastic it was impossible to say no.

"I never thought about that," she admitted.

"And it's not something I've done, not in this way. If you don't like it, don't feel obligated. It's just a suggestion, and I'm fine with either making something or picking it up at the store." Despite what he said, his dark blue eyes shimmered with excitement.

"I like it," she replied earnestly, envisioning it just as easily as he seemed to. "It's something a little different, and that might be good if I'm trying to attract attention to this place." It sounded like the sort of thing Jenna would approve of.

"Great! I've just got to get out into the woods and find the right piece. It might take a bit of time, but I'm sure I can. As for tonight—"

"I want to go." Her mouth said the words without

her permission, but she knew she felt them honestly.

"You want to help pick it out?" Pax pointed vaguely to himself and then to the door.

"Yeah. I mean, something like that will be the center of the house. I like to think I should have some sort of say in it." It was also a great excuse to get away from her office and from that awful appointment she'd just finished. She was in her head too much about it, and some fresh air would do her some good. "How about right now?"

There was that crinkle at the corner of his eyes again, though his smile was much bigger than it'd been when he'd been standing on her porch. "Let's go."

It took only a couple of minutes to change her shoes and grab her coat, and then Pax was holding the passenger side door of his truck open for her. She smiled at him in thanks, and she was surprised at how intimate it felt to sink down into the warm leather interior. The cab wasn't full of loose tools and sawdust like she expected. It was actually fairly clean, and it smelled like freshly cut wood mixed with the more subtle scent of his cologne.

As they drove away, Carrie wondered if she actually cared that much about picking out the handrail or if she just wanted an excuse to spend time with Pax. She glanced at his profile as he concentrated on the road. The slightly heavy brow, the long straight line of his nose, and those incredibly kissable lips. What did it matter what her motivation was?

12

"What is this place?" Carrie trudged along beside him, looking around with interest.

Pax smiled slightly to himself as he walked next to her. She'd moved quickly as soon as she'd decided she was coming with him for this task. For a reason he couldn't quite explain, he was pleased to see that she'd produced a pair of waterproof hiking boots in a matter of seconds. They looked good on her, and she looked good out there in the woods. Her eyes were the same color as the leaves in midsummer, bringing life to the cold winter forest that surrounded them. The dark curls of her hair reminded him of the wild vines that wrapped themselves around the trees. It was easy to lose himself in her.

He hadn't been certain it would be that way. Pax knew Carrie wouldn't have been out of line at all if she'd railed at him when he'd shown up, demanding to know why he'd associated her own lack of a relationship with her work. After all, he was the one who'd pulled her into his arms and made love to her on the rug and then never said another word about it, as though that evening had never happened.

But neither had she.

He adjusted his grip on the compact, battery-operated chainsaw he'd picked for this particular expedition. They wouldn't be felling a full-sized tree, after all. This would likely be either a thick vine or a branch, one that had been forced by the elements to grow anything but straight. It wouldn't take much to cut through the few inches of diameter they'd need for a handrail.

"It's my family's property," he finally answered, realizing he was getting so lost in his thoughts, he was hardly a part of reality anymore. Carrie had that effect on him. "We've owned it for generations. We're right on the border of it here, where it adjoins some neighboring land, but we own everything else you can see." He swung his arms to indicate most of the panorama.

He could tell her. It was a more tempting thought

now that they were out there alone, with nothing but the wilderness around them. He could tell her right then and there exactly why he'd focused only on the house and the necessary repairs instead of the energy that crackled so determinedly between them. Pax opened his mouth, wondering what might happen if he summoned the words. They'd start, and then he'd never be able to stop them. And what would she do? Laugh at him, probably. "I can't love you because I'm not human" sounded like the sorriest excuse in the book. And then what? She'd think he was crazy, and she'd hire someone else to finish the house for her. What would be his excuse to see her then?

The space between her brows scrunched together a bit, something he noticed she did when she was thinking. "I'm sorry to ask a question like this, but why do you have so much wooded land here if you're in the logging industry?"

"No, it's okay." It did strike him as a little odd, but then again, how would Carrie know how they operated? "We do cut timber for a living, but for quite a long time now, we've been select cutting. Razing down everything on the acreage means taking trees that aren't good for lumber or other uses, and then there's nothing left. With our methods, the trees that stay behind are at all different ages, and the land can be cut for timber multiple times profitably."

"I didn't realize." Her smile grew a little more. "Can I assume that's better for the environment as well as your ledger book?"

"You can. Everything from carbon neutralization and erosion to forest fires. It keeps more habitat in place for wildlife, too." *Wildlife like me,* he thought. Carrie might be enchanted by their logging methods, but she'd undoubtedly be far less captivated if she knew about the other side of him.

Even now, he felt his bear surfacing. It often did when she was nearby, but it wasn't simply hungering to be near her. It was on guard. He glanced around, but the only thing worth noting was that they didn't have a lot of daylight left. Pax highly doubted they'd come across the perfect piece of wood for the railing that day, but if that called for another walk in the woods with a beautiful woman, he wouldn't turn it down.

"Oh, look."

He turned to where she pointed, expecting to find that perfect piece of timber he'd just been hoping didn't exist. Instead, she pointed to a tall, straight birch tree ahead of them. "I don't think that's going to work."

"No, look," she laughed as she moved closer. She lifted her hand to trace the outline of a heart that'd been carved into the tree. Two sets of initials were engraved inside it, with the pale, papery bark serving as a contrast to the darker wood underneath. "Do you know who would've done this?"

"D.T. and R.M." Pax smiled. "I think I might, but it's pretty old at this point." It was hard to imagine someone like Dean being that mushy, but judging by how far up from the ground the heart had grown at this point, he would've been just a teenager. Just like most young romances, it was one that hadn't lasted.

"Isn't it sweet?" Her fingertip lingered on the bottom point of the heart, and a trace of a smile curled her lips. "This is the kind of thing people stop doing for each other once they've been in a relationship for a while. We work hard when we want to keep someone, but then it just sort of stops. As soon as we think there's no longer any reason to worry about our partners leaving us, we stop trying. Of course, that's when people do end up leaving us."

"Is that why you talk so much about bonding in your book?" Pax watched her fingers slide down the rough surface of the tree, wishing they were trailing down his body instead. She was such a strange woman, so completely human, yet unlike any of the others he'd met. The more he spent time with her, the less there was of that wall around her.

"You read my book?"

Her stunned words froze him. Pax's gaze remained on the tree instead of looking at her. Apparently, he'd lost a bit of whatever wall he'd been putting up as well, or he never would've slipped up and told her that. "Well, um, I mean, I skimmed it. I was just curious about it." He could still feel her eyes on him, so he turned to find that she looked just as soft and luscious as ever. Her lips were velvety, her eyes warm. She turned him into liquid gold on the inside. "Is that all right?"

She blinked and shook her head a little, breaking the spell. "Of course, it is. You publish a book so people will read it, right? I was just surprised, that's all."

Pax turned back toward the path, knowing they were heading into dangerous territory if they stood there and stared into each other's eyes much longer. "You figured no one from the speed dating event would be willing to read an intelligent book that asks you to actually think?"

"I never said that," she corrected quickly. "In fact, I *hope* anyone who was there that night will read my book if there's any chance that it'll help them."

"You really do like helping people, don't you?"

Carrie tipped her head to the side. She reached a hand back to adjust her hair, her fingers sinking into the curls, and Pax wondered if she was buying time to come up with the right answer. Was she still thinking about the judgmental way he'd questioned her therapy sessions? He hoped not.

"I do," she finally said. "I guess that might seem silly. People's personal lives are their own business, and I think most of us are justified in leaving them to it. But I've always been so fascinated by what makes one person want to be with another, and then what makes them stay or leave. It's probably very similar to what makes you want to work with your hands all the time, or the way you must feel about these woods."

"What if I don't feel anything about them?" He was provoking her, and he knew it. He also knew it probably made him sound like a complete ass, but maybe that was a test in and of itself. God, why did she turn him into a buffoon every two seconds?

"Oh, you do," she replied easily, not bothered by his challenging tone. "I could see it all over you as soon as we got here."

Pax popped his head back a little in surprise before he turned his eyes away from the trees to look at her once again. "Really? And what does it look like?"

There was that warmth in her face again, that enticing look as her eyes flicked over his face and she let her real spirit shine through. "The way you feel about it might be easier to describe than the way it looks to someone else. It's like there's a part of you that's been reaching out for it the whole time, and it's finally satisfied. Like you're home."

His bear spun inside of him as it called out to her. Pax could've stopped his hand as it reached up, the back of his finger brushing her cheek, but he didn't bother trying. He didn't want to stop himself anymore. Pax wasn't even entirely sure of when they'd stopped walking again, or when they'd stepped so close to each other that their bodies were separated by mere inches of chilly February air, air that was filled with the buzzing energy that constantly pulsed between them. Close enough that nothing would stop them, not if they really wanted this. His body surged, and Pax didn't care what she was anymore. She could be a shifter, a human, or a goddamn alien for all he cared, as long as he could be this close to her forever.

Cradling her cheek in one hand, his other closed on her hip. He could feel the heaviness of his eyelids as he studied her mouth, the jolt of electricity that sizzled through his tongue and down through his body as he longed to kiss her. "And what about you? Where do you feel most at home?"

Carrie's eyes were trained on his lips as well, and he could feel her heart thudding under his hands as she dragged her gaze up to his eyes. "Right h—what was that?" She snapped her head to the side, breaking the spell.

Pax reluctantly turned away from her, but only because he'd heard it, too. There were always noises in the woods of some kind. Twigs rubbed against each other in the wind, and branches that had grown weak would snap and fall. Squirrels sounded remarkably like humans as they hopped through the leaf litter. But this had been a more definitive crack, like something—or someone—stepping on a stick. "There shouldn't be anyone else out here right now."

"Maybe it was just my imagination." Her voice was shaking. Ever so slightly, but still shaking.

There was nothing Pax would've liked more than to dismiss all her concerns and pick up where they left off, but he'd heard it, too. More importantly, his bear was on high alert now. Pax wished he was in that form because his senses would be far more acute. He'd have no problem discerning exactly what they heard and in what direction it'd come. As a human, he could only guess. The simple fact that his bear was roaring at him from inside, however, told him all he needed to know.

It was confirmed a moment later when a large, hulking form arose over the next ridgetop. The fur was dark and dense, and its claws sank easily into the soft loam under its wide paws. It wasn't Dean or Evan, and it definitely wasn't James. In fact, this bear wasn't from his clan at all. Pax's chest heaved as he tried to figure out the right thing to say to Carrie.

But then the creature lifted its nose into the air, its dark eyes settling determinedly on her.

13

Her guts churned. Adrenaline gushed through her veins and made her fingers shake. Carrie stared at the enormous beast as it lumbered closer. It was so close! What was she supposed to do? Desperately, Carrie tried to remember all the things she'd been told about encountering a bear. She could clearly recall the face of the handsome trail guide her Girl Scout troop had followed along on one summer Saturday, but not what he'd said. Didn't he say something about bears? She hadn't worried about it in so long, not while living in town. Things were going to be different in Oregon, though, and she'd skimmed an article online. Her memory of it was just as useless. Was she supposed to run away or stay put?

Be loud or be quiet? Was it different depending on the kind of bear? Indecision battled itself in her brain.

"Pax," she whispered. Carrie didn't know what the hell she thought he could do. She couldn't even bring herself to turn her head and look at him, because that would mean taking her eyes off the very creature that might be preparing to have her for dinner.

"It's okay." He was doing something. She could hear him moving.

As the bear moved closer and all the air left her lungs, she wasn't so sure. It lifted its snout into the air, its nostrils flaring. Was it smelling her? What did it *want* her to smell like? Her stomach curled around her spine and shivered.

Slowly, as though it'd found exactly what it was looking for, the grizzly brought its nose back down. Its eyes bored into her. Their brown depths were terrifying, yet mesmerizing. Carrie had never seen anything quite like it before. This wasn't the bored stare of an animal in the zoo, but an intelligent creature. *This is how I'm going to die.*

The bear locked its gaze on her, its shoulders hunching slightly as its claws dug into the dirt. Its muscles bunched and stretched as it lunged toward her, mouth open, exposing its sharp white teeth and saliva dripping from its lips. It was coming straight at her.

There was no time to move. No time to run. This was a creature made for killing, and it was going to do just that.

Something slammed into her left side, knocking her to the ground. Carrie put her arms up to protect her head as she rolled into the leaf litter. What little breath she had left in her lungs came rushing out. When she looked up, she could hardly believe what she was seeing.

The bear that had charged her was still standing there, mere feet away. Its mouth gaped open as it roared, its hot breath sweeping against her body. But it didn't attack. It didn't clamp its jaws down on her ankle and drag her off into the woods, but only because a *second bear* was staring it down.

This one stood next to her, its feet so close, Carrie could reach out and touch them if she could get her own body to cooperate and start moving again. It bellowed at the attacker as it took a few steps forward, challenging it. This new bear, wherever it'd come from, was trying to chase off the first. It snarled and raged, and when the first creature snapped out with its jaws, it charged. A squeal of shock escaped Carrie's lips as the two bodies slammed into each other. The reverberation rippled through the ground, but they didn't even seem to notice. Claws and teeth raked against fur.

Carrie's heels dug into the ground as she tried to push herself backward, away from the fray. Panic was still guiding her body, though, keeping her from getting the hell out of there. "Pax?" He didn't answer, yet she couldn't tear herself away from the gruesome scene before her.

This second bear, the one that was either protecting her or claiming her for its own dinner, was larger than the first. It rammed its head into its enemy's jaw. Then, like a boxer taking advantage of its opponent, it shoved again while the first suffered from the impact. There was more growling and snarling, the noise completely filling the woods. Carrie thought at last that it might be over, that the first bear might be giving up, but he slashed out with one paw and split the thick fur of his foe. It was a long gash, but not enough to stop him. The second bear came back harder, sinking its teeth into the first's shoulder and ripping back. Blood gushed out onto the ground, hot and steaming.

The scene blurred. Carrie was suddenly no

longer sure of which bear was which. She thought the second one was slightly paler, but now she couldn't tell. The parts of her body weren't working in sync anymore. Her brain said to run, but her muscles wouldn't cooperate. She knew she needed to breathe, but her lungs refused to pull in any air. Carrie blinked, aware now that a blackness was seeping in around the edges of her vision. She tried to fight it. She knew she should. There was nothing she could do, and the blackness took over.

"Carrie. Carrie. Come back to me."

She didn't want to open her eyes. It was safer in the darkness. But her body was starting to remind her of just how cold it was getting, and that voice was tempting.

"Please, Carrie."

She lifted her lids to find Pax hovering over her. His eyes were full of concern. Pale blue winter sky surrounded him, broken up by gently swaying treetops. Warm hands touched her face.

"There you are." He let out a breath that was either exasperation or relief.

She didn't have the energy to find out. "What the hell?"

That earned her a laugh. "What the hell is right. Are you okay? I don't see any broken bones or bleeding. Did you hit your head?"

"No. I think I passed out. Adrenaline and I don't get along well." As he helped her sit up, she tried to stitch it all back together again. There was the bear and then another bear.

"That served you well, then. If you'd tried to fight back, you might have a lot more than a few bumps and bruises. Come on. I'll get you back to the truck."

"Yeah, just...give me a minute." Carrie allowed him to help her to her feet, but the shock of losing consciousness wasn't something she could get past easily. She leaned against a tree as she waited for her head to clear.

"Of course. Take all the time you need." The cords in his neck were tense as he looked around.

"You don't think they'll come back, do you?" Shit, she'd be dead for sure if they did, especially if running away was the right thing to do.

But he shook his head quickly. "No, I don't think they will."

"Wait, what about you?" she asked, suddenly realizing that though she'd been aware of Pax's presence throughout the ordeal, she hadn't actually seen him. "Are you all right?"

"I'm fine. Don't worry about me." He brushed his fingers against the bottom hem of her jacket, whisking away a few fragments of dead leaves.

Carrie could tell something was going on with him. Of course, he'd lost that happy, contented feeling she'd sensed in him when they'd first entered the woods. Encountering a bear would certainly do that to someone, particularly if it was two bears. "I don't think I quite understand what happened."

Now his eyes came back up to hers, but only for a moment. "What do you remember?"

She pulled in a deep breath, still trying to calm her shaking body. "The bear showed up, and it attacked. Then another bear knocked me to the side and fought it. I don't really remember anything else." She racked her brain, still feeling like something was missing.

"That's the long and short of it." He picked up the chainsaw, which at some point had fallen on the ground, and wrapped his other arm around her waist. "Are you about ready to head back?"

Carrie opened her mouth to protest, to tell him that he didn't need to fuss over her and that she was fine. But as she pushed herself up off the tree trunk and straightened, she wasn't completely sure she was fine at all. Her heart still thundered, and she felt like she could simply lay on the ground, curl into a ball, and go to sleep. "Yeah, I guess so."

"Just let me know if you start to feel faint again." His left hand gripped her hip tightly, the length of his forearm wrapped around her waist.

Yes, she absolutely knew she wanted to fall asleep now, but only if she could do so right there in his arms. It might have been that second bear that saved her life, but she felt the shield of protection coming from Pax. She was falling harder than she'd ever meant to, that was for sure. She had no choice but to put her own arm around him, looping it underneath his jacket so she could feel the heat of his muscled back against her. "Why did that other bear get involved and save us?"

Pax shrugged, a roll of his shoulder that nestled her a little more snugly against his ribs. "Maybe we got in the way of some dispute that was already going on."

"Ah." That made sense, at least. More sense than anything else did at the moment. "It was strange. I know it all happened quickly, so fast that I didn't even know how to react. But I could see it all so clearly, like it was in high-res slow motion."

"The kind of thing people pay extra for when they're watching football," Pax replied lightly.

"Very funny." She didn't let go of his arm or push him away for trying to turn this into a joking matter, though. Instead, Carrie closed her eyes for a moment to indulge herself in the way the inside of his arm felt around her waist. Strong. Steady. Like it belonged there. Those were just the sort of thoughts that happened after someone got incredibly scared. Carrie had studied more than just marital relationships when she'd been in college, and she knew there was some psychology behind what was happening. She wasn't sure she cared, and she *was* sure that she wanted him to keep his arm around her.

"I'm guessing this is the first time you've ever run into a wild animal face-to-face like that?" He shifted his grip on the chainsaw, but he looked to be carrying it and helping her with ease.

"Anything other than a raccoon, yeah."

"Then you're probably just a little freaked out. I'm sure that would happen for anyone." Pax slowed as they hit a slightly steeper part of the trail, stepping carefully and making sure Carrie could get down the incline without any problems.

Her blood pressure was coming back up to

normal now that she was up and walking again. The truth was she didn't need his support at all anymore. She simply wanted it. Carrie pressed her tongue against the back of her teeth, wishing she could make up her mind to either want to pursue this strange man of the woods or just stay the hell away from him. "You weren't scared?"

He didn't say anything for a moment. "Something like that, anyway."

She bit the inside of her cheek to keep from smiling, figuring that he was just trying to be macho. Carrie was content to let him be just that because he was certainly far more capable than she was when it came to anything that had to do with house repairs, the woods, and apparently, wildlife. She was finally starting to feel like the bear incident was behind them, and when she looked around her the next time, she no longer felt like she was going to see yet another furry brown face staring out at her through the thin winter underbrush.

Instead she saw something else. "That's it!"

He paused, his back stiffening a bit, but she felt him relax when he saw what she pointed to. "I think you're right. Let's find a place for you to sit while I measure it."

"No, I'll be okay. Really," she added when he shot her a dubious look.

Pax slowly let go of her and unclipped a measuring tape from his belt.

Carrie instantly missed his touch. The absence was made even greater by the cold that invaded her skin as soon as his warmth was missing, but she zipped her jacket up a little higher. As though that could possibly make up for it. "Is there anything I can do?"

He was pushing through the brush, getting a good look at the long, curved piece of wood. "Just tell me for sure if you want it, but I don't think we'll find anything better. It's actually a whole tree. This other one fell on top of it when it was very young, and it's been growing like this ever since. I'll just have to strip off the bark and send it to the kiln to be dried, and we're good to go."

"Looks good to me." The potential new handrailing certainly did, but Carrie had to admit that he did, too. Pax moved with ease and confidence as he cut the tree, using the small chainsaw as though it were a part of him. She knew that he'd been doing this for a living for a long time, but it was still something altogether different to witness it.

She could almost hear her sister's voice inside

her head. *Since when did you fall for tough, rugged guys with callouses on their hands instead of artists, writers, or musicians?* Carrie smiled. Pax wasn't the kind of guy who'd ever been her type. She'd tried to fight it so hard, but she was starting to think he was absolutely her type now.

14

Chase let out a low whistle as he stepped in. "This is a pretty nice place. I'm surprised you're having to spend so much time fixing it up. Or is it just that you want to spend time with the woman who owns it?"

"This is the best-looking part of the house." Pax shot his cousin a look as he closed the door behind them. "Don't make me regret bringing you here. And it's a good thing Carrie is meeting with Jenna right now; otherwise, she probably would've heard that." Pax knew from experience that the walls weren't all that thick. That would change once he could blow some extra insulation in, but that was just one of many things on a long To-Do list.

"I wouldn't normally say anything, except I

figured there had to be something that was pulling you back to this house so much. Something you like even more than your tools." Chase waggled his dark eyebrows.

"You can be such a kid sometimes, you know that?" Pax punched him in the arm. "I'm surprised Jenna puts up with you."

"Me, too, but I'll take it. I guess this is where the railing is going in unless you've got some other dangerous staircase hiding around here." Chase gestured toward the stairs.

Pax had already spent some time sanding where the balusters had broken off. He'd created new ones in his woodshop, which would reflect both the natural beauty of the new handrail and recall the older style the house was originally based on. It had been a bit of a challenge to come up with something he liked, and he'd spent far too much time at his lathe, but overall he was satisfied. At least with the work. "This is the one. I figured we'd get all the tools in, and then we can grab everything else out of the back of the truck."

"Works for me." Chase headed back outside.

The afternoon was bright and refreshing. There was just the barest hint that spring would be coming along soon, even though the temperatures were staying cold. Pax glanced at the wooded acre that surrounded the house, and it brought his mind back to that encounter in his family's woods. Hell, everything made him think about that. He'd worked quickly to get the handrail ready, and even though finding that particular piece of timber wasn't an unhappy memory, it was still associated with that day. "How are things going down at The Warehouse?" he asked to give himself something else to think about.

Chase put down the tailgate and lifted one end of the handrail, waiting for Chase to grab the other end. He smiled. "Pretty damn good, actually. Everyone who said it was going to be a complete failure in comparison to all the wineries around here can kiss my ass. I've had to hire more staff and increase the hours we're open just to accommodate everyone."

"That's what happens when your mate is a master marketer." Pax lifted his end of the handrail.

Some men might have a hard time getting such a large, awkward piece of material up the porch stairs and in through the door. Chase had spent most of his life working for Thompson and Sons before he'd opened the brewery, though, which meant both of them were used to heavy labor that had to be synchronized to get any results.

"You can't give her *all* the credit," Chase said with a grin as he fell into step with his cousin. "Not that she doesn't deserve a ton of it. I don't think it would be as impressive and successful without her. I guess she's consulting for this therapist lady, too."

Pax felt his mouth tighten at such an odd descriptor as he backed in the front door. It made sense for someone who didn't know Carrie, he supposed, but not for him. Carrie wasn't just 'some therapist lady.' She was so much more. "It sounds like she's setting her up for quite the business venture herself."

"Yeah, you said this is going to be a bed and breakfast, right?"

"That's the plan." Pax knew it'd be a while yet before it was ready. Every time he finished one project, he added another to his list. He didn't mind. It meant he was always busy and was able to see Carrie. The only problem was figuring out how he felt about seeing her.

"Are you brooding again?"

"What?" Pax laid the handrail carefully down on the stairs where it would be ready to put in place as soon as the balusters were installed.

"I was just asking when you're going to come over for dinner, but you just muttered something about wood instead." Chase gave him a hard look.

"I'm just distracted, that's all." That was one way of putting it. He was definitely distracted, but at this point, he couldn't tell if it was Carrie that was distracting him from the rest of his life or the other way around.

His cousin nodded. "That's what I hear. Even Dad mentioned it to me, and you know how he is."

Unfortunately, Pax did. James didn't talk about personal issues unless they really bothered him, and he thought something major was going on. "I don't suppose he's still blaming me for that incident that almost killed Dean."

"No. He's been talking with Chris a lot about what they can possibly do. They both know that the Ballards will just deny it. But I think that's actually what made Dad bring up the stuff with you. You might not be making mistakes on the job, but he can tell something is going on."

Pax rolled his eyes. The last thing he needed was for James to start speculating to everyone else in the clan about him. James Thompson wasn't much of a talker, so if he did open his mouth, the others would listen. But would they understand?

He paused, thinking about Chase and his relationship with Jenna. It wasn't as though Chase had been the first clan member to fall in love with a human, but he was probably the person Pax was closest to. Pax picked up a bottle of wood glue. "Does it ever bother you that Jenna is a human?"

"Whoa." Chase was visibly startled by the question, his shoulders rolling back and his eyes widening. "It doesn't bother me in the least. Does it bother you?"

"No, no. That's not why I'm asking." Pax pulled in a deep breath, knowing that if he let this out, there would be no getting it back. The information would be out there in the world. Maybe that was for the best. "I just...I know that you and Jenna are meant to be together. Anyone who looks at the two of you can see that. And I know that other men like us have made it work, as Tyler did with Liz. I guess I'm just wondering if you have any regrets now that you've made the decision. If there are any differences that the two of you can't get past because you're different species."

Chase picked up a baluster and handed it to Pax, where he crouched on the stairs. "This is an odd question coming from you. As I recall, you encouraged me to go for it with Jenna. I believe 'go after her and give yourself a chance to be heard' was part of your sage advice."

Accepting the baluster, Pax pointed at the toolbox. "Give me that mallet."

"Only if you're not going to hit me with it," his cousin joked.

"Only if you don't deserve it." Pax felt the wry smile on his face. It was ironic that he'd given that advice to Chase, especially since that was exactly what he needed right now. "I'm not sure I knew what I was talking about back then."

"It worked for us," Chase reminded him. "I can't even imagine what life would be like without Jenna and Alexander. That kid means the world to us."

Pax sighed as he put the next baluster in place. "That's true, but I think sometimes it's easier to see these things from the outside. You don't get all mixed up with all the second-guessing and doubts. It was obvious that you and Jenna had great chemistry together. That was the only thing I needed to know."

"And what about you and...wait. Who, exactly, are you talking about?" Chase twirled one of the balusters in his hand to examine the woodwork, but he glanced up at his cousin for the answer.

"I never actually said that I was talking about anyone specific," Pax reminded him. "I just asked how you were feeling these days about living with a human."

"Nice evasion, there. And I'm not just living with Jenna. We're not roommates, and it's not the same thing as having one. There's more understanding than just splitting the rent or figuring out who's night it is to order pizza. There's that deep connection that transcends all that. It makes the other bullshit not matter. Now, who is it?" He held the baluster out of reach while he waited for his answer.

"Seriously, man?"

"Seriously."

"Fine. It's Carrie. The woman who owns this house. Now don't gloat at me because your suspicions were right." He snagged the baluster from Chase's hands and put it in place, feeling his cheeks burning.

"I'm not going to gloat. And you don't have to tell me," he said quickly when Pax started to open his mouth. "I won't mention it to Jenna, either. I'm sure she'd love to hear it, but I won't tell her. Or maybe I won't tell her as long as you promise to actually do something about this."

Pax chuckled, fairly certain his cousin was kidding. "You're a shithead."

With the last of the uprights installed, it was time

to put the handrail in place. Pax was grateful that they no longer spoke as they carefully picked it up and lowered it on the balusters. The tops of the spindles glided in just as he'd planned, and the end of the handrail butted perfectly up against the newel post. "Perfect. Just a few screws, and we're almost done."

But Chase wasn't quite done with the conversation. "Do you think she's the one?"

With the structure well enough in place that it wasn't going anywhere, Pax sat back on the stair tread. "That's what's been getting to me so much, I think. I keep focusing on the fact that she's human, and I think that's important, but that's not all of it. I'm ready to settle down. I told myself that I needed to find someone to be with because I didn't want to be one of these grumpy old men who'd been a bachelor his entire life. I didn't think Carrie could possibly be my mate because she's not a shifter, but the way I feel about her, I have to wonder. And then I have to wonder if I'm just imagining that I feel that way so that I'll feel like I found my soulmate." It was a frustrating thing to admit.

They were silent for a time while they finished working. There was something relaxing in the simple sounds of the tools and in knowing that he was accomplishing something by putting this railing in. It meant he'd also worry a little less about Carrie. His thoughts always came around to her, whether he was in her house or not.

When they'd finished, and there was nothing left to do but shake the railing a little and comment on just how sturdy it was, Chase closed the top of the toolbox. "I think you need to tell her."

Pax braced one hand on his hip and the other on the railing. "I don't know if I can. I see her almost every day. I've had dozens of opportunities, but I haven't said a damn word." Hell, he'd even had sex with her. It was easier to literally get naked in front of her than to bare his soul.

"She hasn't said it, either," Chase pointed out, "but it sounds like there must be something you both feel, or you wouldn't even be worried about it. Just tell her. What's the worst thing that can happen?"

"I've been through a few scenarios," Pax muttered. But his cousin was right. She could say no. She could fire him from the remodeling job. It would hurt, but he'd live. "You're probably right."

"That does happen on occasion," he joked. Chase glanced at the clock on the mantel. "I'd better be getting home, unless there's something else you need help with."

"No, thanks. I've just got a few things I need to finish up tonight, and then I'll be packing up. Thanks for the assist, though."

"Sure."

When Chase was gone, Pax sat on the stairs. He was technically by himself, but never truly alone when he was in Carrie's house. Her scent lingered in the air, and he could feel just what it'd be like to have her sitting there on the stairs next to him. Pax wasn't sure why things had to be so difficult when it came to finding a mate. Older shifters often talked about it as though it were simple, but he had a feeling they were so distanced from the event itself, they didn't remember it clearly. Maybe Chase was right, but that didn't mean he had to tell her right away. It wouldn't hurt anything to mull it over for just a bit longer.

In the meantime, he had enough work to keep himself occupied well into the evening. Instead, he pulled out his pocket knife, flicked it open, and pressed the tip into the underside of the new railing.

15

"Come on in." Carrie held the door open for Emery. She smiled warmly at him, but he didn't look too pleased.

"Thanks for fitting me in so quickly," he mumbled as he came in the door. Emery looked even more furtive and uncomfortable than he had before, even though he'd already had a session alone to get used to the place. He hovered in front of the couch, looking stiff.

"It's not a problem. I try to make accommodations for my clients whenever I can. It's not unusual for someone to see if I can squeeze them in last minute. Have a seat." Carrie gestured at the couch once again before having a seat herself.

He hesitated, looking like he might bolt out the door instead of sitting. Finally, after he practically vibrated in place for a moment, he sat stiffly. He was all sharp angles, though, not relaxing the way he had last time.

"Where would you like to start?" she asked gently, sensing that there was definitely something wrong. He looked so anxious and jumpy that she wondered if someone had mocked him for coming to therapy. It wasn't uncommon, even among adults. "Did you tell Jessica how your previous session went?"

Emery nodded. "She wasn't all that happy about it."

It was hard to keep herself from frowning. Carrie felt their last appointment had gone well, and that her new client would have lots of positive information to bring back to his fiancée. "Why don't you tell me more about that?"

He was sweating, and he looked pale. He didn't answer.

"Emery? Are you feeling all right? I can get you a cold bottle of water if you'd like."

He yanked his brows down as though this was a major decision. "Sure," he finally answered. "That'd be good."

"I'll be right back." Carrie set down her notepad and opened the office door. She realized halfway through the house that she still had her pen in her hand, and she rolled the cold metal barrel around between her fingers. It felt good, calming in a way, and that was exactly why she was getting this cold water for Emery. Something about the chill always took the edge off anxiety.

The kitchen was still in the pitiful state it'd been in when she'd first seen the place. Carrie hadn't paid all that much attention to it at the time, being more concerned with just getting a roof over her head than anything else. But now that she knew Pax was creating an entirely new set of cabinets, she couldn't wait to see them. It was tempting to ask him if she could come to his place and see how they were coming along. Not that she'd know anything about it or that she had any concerns. No, the truth was that she just wanted to learn more about him.

He'd been weighing on her mind even more than usual after their hike and encounter with the two bears. It'd been so strange, and it'd come as one hell of a shock that she still hadn't quite gotten over, but it was more exciting to focus on the way Pax had been so sweet and supportive. The new railing, now installed, looked absolutely gorgeous. That alone made it worth it, she supposed, but having his arms around her again was even better.

"Here you go," she said as she came back into the office. She bent to set the bottle of water on the coffee table in front of Emery. "Now tell me a little about Jessica."

Emery didn't respond. He leaped up off the couch, moving so quickly that Carrie didn't even have a chance to straighten up. He spun her around and pulled her against him, his left arm pinning hers to her body. She could feel his chest heaving against her back. Something cold pressed against her throat. Instinctively, Carrie tipped her head back to get away from the sharp edge of the blade, but there was little she could do. He was young and strong, and he'd caught her completely off guard. "Emery, what is this all about?"

"Tell me about the next contract," he said through his teeth, his breath hot on the back of her head.

Saliva was pooling in her mouth, but she didn't dare swallow. Not with that knife right there, waiting for blood. "I'm not sure what contract you mean, but I would like to help you, Emery. If you let me go, we can talk about this calmly."

He wasn't going to be persuaded so easily. Emery tightened his grip, his breathing coming faster. "You know exactly what I'm talking about!"

They'd gone over this sort of thing during her education and training. Sometimes people got a little too edgy, and they did things they shouldn't. Carrie had listened, trying to make sure she was fully prepared for any such situation. It'd never happened. Not in all her years of practicing. The worst had been some arguments, yelling, or slammed doors. But never a knife to her throat.

Still, she knew humans better than she did bears. That didn't make them any less scary. Carrie thought about the way she'd reacted when she'd seen the big beast in the woods. She'd been too terrified to do much of anything. Her blood rushed through her veins, carrying copious amounts of adrenaline with it once again. Passing out wasn't going to do her any good this time. She had to be stronger.

"Emery." She used his name to keep a connection to him, though she wasn't sure it would help. "Emery, I really don't know what contract you mean. If you could explain it to me, I'd be happy to help. You don't have to do this to get my help."

"Don't play with me," he growled. His breath was

hissing in and out between his teeth now, almost as though he were in pain. "He's here almost every fucking day, alone with you. I've been watching, and I know. Don't pretend you're stupid or like he doesn't talk to you. Tell me what he's told you and who the next contract is with."

Emery's left arm was holding her so hard now, Carrie's left hand was falling asleep and she could barely breathe. She felt like her brain was rattling around inside her skull as she tried to figure out what he was talking about. "Pax?"

"Yes, of course, Pax! Don't play with me, bitch! Tell me what you know!"

"I don't know anything!" She gasped as the knife pressed against her. Emery was scaring her, and now he knew it. She'd given him the upper hand by getting frustrated. Contracts? What the hell kind of business was Pax in on the side?

"Listen, lady. I'm serious. You're smart, and I'm sure you've figured that out by now. Just tell me what Pax told you, and I'll leave. That's what you want, right?"

"Emery, I swear I don't know what you're talking about. Pax is here a lot, yes. He's working on my house. He's remodeling it. That's the extent of things."

His laugh wasn't a humorous one. "That's it? That's why you were out for your cutesy little walk in the woods, exchanging glances? Come on. I know better than that."

Alarm bells clanged in her head. This guy wasn't just freaking out over his upcoming nuptials. There was something significant going on with him—more than she could probably help him with—if he'd taken to following her around. "Emery, you've got to be able to see that this isn't working. I honestly don't know what kind of contract you're talking about. Just let me go, and we'll sit down and talk. Just the two of us."

He bobbed the tip of the knife up and down, making the edge scrape against her skin with a dry, sickening sound. "Fine, you want me to be that blunt? Then tell me who the Thompsons are talking to for their next timber contract. That's what I need to know, and I'm sure your little boyfriend has told you all about it."

"Timber? That's what this is about? Emery, I really don't know anything. Like I said, Pax is just remodeling my house on the side. The only thing I know about timber is what little he told me about it when we went to pick out the wood for the handrail, which you obviously already know about it. And he's not my boyfriend." She wasn't sure if the correction would be good or bad for her, but it was worth the risk.

"Tell me, or you'll get to see what your blood looks like all over this couch." Emery cranked his arm down even tighter.

Carrie's eyes darted around the room, looking for anything she could use as a weapon. There had to be some way she could defend herself. For once, Pax wasn't there to help her. She couldn't remember what time he would show up since his schedule always varied a bit. There was no chance of holding Emery off long enough to hope that he or anyone else would show up. She tightened her free hand.

Her fountain pen was still there. The heat of her hand had chased away all that cold comfort. Carrie ran her thumb down the barrel. She'd left it uncapped, which wasn't something she normally would've done. Right now, though, she didn't give two shits about whether or not the ink dried out. She didn't know if she could do this, but it was the only chance she saw. Wrapping her hand tightly around the barrel and putting her thumb on the end, she yanked her free hand up and stabbed down hard.

The steel nib pierced straight through his jeans

and into his thigh. Carrie cringed at the sick feeling, her throat tightening with a gag. Emery screamed, and his knife hand whipped away from her. She yanked the pen back out, ignoring the sick sucking sound, and stabbed again. Her entire body and being told her not to do this, not to hurt another person, but it was overwhelmed by her will to survive. Blood welled up, mixing with a runnel of bright purple ink, and soaked his jeans as he staggered back into the couch.

This was the chance she'd been waiting for. Leaving her pen behind, she turned and went for the door. The office wasn't a large space, but it suddenly felt huge as she tried to get across it. This was like a horrible nightmare, the kind where she couldn't move even though she desperately wanted to.

Chills shivered up her spine as she turned her back on him, knowing he was right there behind her. The coffee table was in her way, and Carrie skirted around it, thinking her path to the door was finally free.

But her foot rolled over something cold and round. The water bottle had fallen off the table at some point while they struggled, sending her hurtling forward, her arms and legs flying uselessly.

She let out a grunt as her knees hit the floor, but she wasn't about to give up.

Carrie reached up for the doorknob just as a hand closed around her ankle.

16

"That's it for the day." James dusted his hands off on his jeans. "We've got everything on this property that we're going to get, and there's not enough daylight to set back up over at the Copelands'. We'll get started there tomorrow."

Pax put his chainsaw in its case and loaded it in the back of the truck. "That went fast."

"You shouldn't mind. It means you get to go play Handyman and Horny Housewife with your lady friend," Dean said with a grin.

"Kiss my ass." Pax considered saying something to him about the heart he and Carrie had found carved in that tree, but Dean would just turn around and use it against him as evidence that he wanted to work on more than Carrie's house. It reminded him of something else that needed to be taken care of, though, and he stepped over to his uncle. "Did Chris say anything about what I told you?"

"Not much. He said he'd look into it. His son is sick, though, so I'm sure he's preoccupied with that."

"Mm." An unsettled feeling came over Pax. He didn't like the idea of leaving something like this unresolved. "I don't know exactly who it was, but it had to be one of the Ballards. They were on our land. You'd think Chris would want to jump right on this, especially since the bastard nearly exposed our secret to a human."

James had been loading his clipboard and a few other things into the passenger side of his truck. Now he shut the door and leaned against it as he gave Pax a solemn look. "True, but you could be blamed for that just as easily. Everyone in our clan sees that land as a safe place to be, regardless of what form we're in. You shouldn't have taken her there."

Anger flushed through his veins at the idea of anyone blaming him or Carrie for this. "How can you say that? If it'd been you or Dean or anyone else in our clan, there would've been nothing more than a bear sighting by a hiker. Carrie might have been a little scared, but we would've left without incident. That asshole attacked her!"

"I know, I know." James pressed his hand through the air in a meager gesture to calm Pax down. "I'm just trying to say there are different ways to look at this. It's not as simple as you'd like to think. I'm sure Chris will talk to old Jacob and get things sorted out. Just be glad you were able to take care of it as discreetly as you were."

"Right." Dissatisfied, Pax finished packing up. He fired up his truck and headed down the hill toward the country roads that would take him back to town. He had the rest of the day off, and though he hadn't made any specific plans, he knew exactly what he'd be doing. The cabinets for Carrie's kitchen were coming along swiftly, and he was eager to tear out the old ones and replace them. He could blast some music and work the rest of the day away.

There was something he wanted to do even more than that, though. The cabinets were a fun project, and they would make Carrie happy, but he wasn't sure how much longer he could go on with this charade. Chase had told him to go for it and just tell Carrie how he felt. It was easy to pretend he had plenty of time, that he wasn't in a hurry. After all, he'd already waited this long to find his life partner.

What were a few more days or weeks without his mate?

It was only that tiny logical part of his mind that felt that way, though. The entirety of him wanted her, his body, mind, soul, and bear. At the last minute, he yanked the truck to the left before he missed the turn that would take him to her house.

He was making it more difficult than it had to be, he knew. Pax wasn't completely blind. He hadn't missed the way she looked at him when she thought he wasn't watching, or how she'd melted against his side as they'd walked through the woods. She obviously felt *something* for him. Hell, he probably could've told her quite some time ago how he felt. Carrie was a logical woman, and she did have all that stuff in her book about accepting people for who they were.

Pax tapped his fingers impatiently as he rolled to a stop at an intersection. There would be no discussion about what color to paint the kitchen or what stain to use on the cabinets. He wouldn't skirt around the real issue at hand by asking her which of the bedrooms they would start on first or if she wanted him to have a go at repairing some of the trim near the back door. He would have her sit with him—wherever that happened to be in this house that he'd come to know so well, he didn't care—and he'd tell her what he really felt.

That meant he'd have to tell her the rest of it. Pax knew it wouldn't be fair, otherwise. Keeping the shifter secret was fine for a date or two, but not for love. Carrie had to know him completely.

All the logic and mental preparation in the world couldn't make him anything less than a nervous wreck as he pulled into her driveway. He frowned when he saw a truck pulled around to the side, where her patients parked. Damn. He hesitated for a moment, his hand on the seat belt buckle. Carrie didn't know he was there. He could simply wait and come back later. His bear had other plans, though. Dark fur prickled at the back of his neck as it threatened to come out and take care of this business for him.

His irregular schedule and her priority towards her clients meant they'd come to the agreement that he could let himself in the front door if she were with someone. Well, so much for not messing around with the trim or the kitchen. He could keep himself busy until she was ready for him, and then they would talk.

Quietly, not wanting to disturb her session, Pax slipped in through the front door. Goosebumps immediately erupted on his skin. He glanced around, not sure why, but then he heard it. An angry, terrified scream rippled through the house, vibrating through the walls and burying itself in his soul like a hatchet. "Emery, please! Stop!"

"Carrie!"

Pax bolted through the house. He didn't need to look around for her now. The wild side of him was taking over completely, and his hearing had already improved even though he was still in his human form. He could hear her sobbing and screaming. Then several thumps. Something was definitely happening.

His hand was hot on the office doorknob as he turned it and flung it open. Carrie was on her knees with her hands twisted behind her. Tears streaked her makeup, but her eyes looked angry more than anything. Her chin was in the air, and a knife was pressed to her throat.

Grinding his teeth together, Pax followed the muscular arm that held the knife up the wild face of a young man with curly hair. He didn't know him in his human form, but he didn't need to. It was the same asshole that had attacked them out in the woods. Pax knew him in the way that only shifters could possibly know each other. It was an animalistic sense that even he couldn't explain if someone had asked him to. "Let her go, Ballard."

The young man grimaced. He flicked his eyes to Pax for only a moment. "I don't think so. I've worked too hard to get this one under control. She's a stubborn little bitch, though."

It was hard to keep himself human. Pax fought it back like a wave of nausea. That was *his mate* this fucker was threatening. It was only the fact that he hadn't told her yet that kept his beast at bay. For now. "What do you want?"

"I have to give you credit, Thompson. I figured your little human mate here would spill the beans as soon as I showed her the knife. I merely asked her a few innocent questions, and she put some ink in my leg for my troubles." Ballard nodded at his leg without taking his eyes off of Pax.

Pax swelled with pride when he saw Carrie's pen sticking out of the man's thigh. He moved his eyes quickly away from it, though, wondering how he would get her out of this situation. Carrie didn't realize that she'd already been in similar circumstances, except the two men she could currently see had been in their ursine forms the last time. "What do you want?" he repeated.

"I just told her she needed to tell me who your

logging operation would be contracting with next, and the bitch refused to say a goddamn word. If you're smart, Thompson, you'll tell me before I finish what I've started." Ballard pressed the tip of his knife a bit harder against the length of Carrie's throat.

It was the tiniest trickle of blood, so little that it would hardly even require a bandage, but it was enough. Pax felt his bear explode out of him. His skull cracked and popped as a muzzle emerged from the front of his face, and his teeth shot like spears from his gums. Though he started forward on human legs, he soon had four bear paws touching the floor. Thick fur bristled out in all directions as he charged his adversary. He briefly saw the look of complete horror on Carrie's face, but he tuned it out. He'd have to deal with the consequences later.

Emery—that's what she'd called him— responded in kind. His knife clattered to the floor near Carrie's knees as he rose, snarling as he let out his animal. Pale eyes changed to a dark brown, but his hair color remained nearly the same as the fur that now sprouted on his skin. His shoulders widened and his back lengthened to accommodate this form. He knocked Carrie to the side as he lurched forward on all fours. If Pax had any doubts before, he now knew for sure this was the same bear he'd encountered in the woods.

Pax met him head-on, the two heavy bodies crashing together. They fell to the side, smashing the coffee table into several pieces. Pax paid no attention to the splinters that dug into his fur as he scrambled to his feet. Emery struggled to get up off the broken table, and his claws sliced through the air. Two of them swiped across Pax's chest, adding to the bloody mess that had already been made on this side of the room. Pax ignored the pain. He pushed himself up so that he stood nearly upright before he let the full weight of his body fall forward onto his enemy.

Emery rolled out of the way just in time, but the maneuver still left him vulnerable. He was young and probably hadn't fought with anyone outside his clan. Pax could smell the tang of his opponent's fear, which drove him even harder. He opened his jaw wide and clamped it down over the fur and loose skin that protected Ballard's neck.

Carrie was still in the back corner of the office. Pax could just see her in his peripheral vision as he battled his rival. Her eyes were wide and her mouth agape as she watched a replay of the scene she'd witnessed in the woods, except this time, the two wild creatures were tearing apart her office.

Get out! Get the hell out of here! Pax's mind reached out to her, but she couldn't hear him. He knew for sure that she was his mate, the one person he was meant to be with. He never would've tried to speak to her telepathically otherwise. But she was human. Shifter mates could hear each other, but even then, it was only when they were in their animal forms.

Emery thrashed around underneath him, his flailing paws sending Carrie's desk chair flying across the room as he freed himself from Pax's grip. He wrenched himself up from the ground to start an attack of his own. Ballard roared as he slammed his head into Pax's shoulder.

The impact was enough to knock Pax off balance. He fell backward into the bookshelf, sending hardbacks raining down on both of them. It was clear that there would be no stopping Emery. He didn't give up after he'd lost in the woods when his shoulder was bleeding so severely, Pax had sent him limping back to his clan. He didn't give up when Pax burst into the office, when he'd had the chance to simply lay the knife down and leave. Even now he was injured, the fur around his neck growing dark with his blood where Pax's teeth had recently sunk through the skin.

With one final bellow of rage, Pax whipped his

head around. He reached out with his jaws, ready to snap them around anything he could get a hold of. Bone hit bone as he bit down on Emery's muzzle. Blood seeped into Pax's mouth, but he couldn't let that stop him. He crunched down harder, feeling the sick crack of bones fracturing, as he used his paw to slash out just under his opponent's chin.

One well-placed claw was enough. It hit Emery's jugular and sent a shower of crimson flowing down onto the floor. Emery shoved his shoulder into Pax several more times, bumping him back against the bookcase, but the efforts swiftly grew weaker. His eyes rolled back in his head and he slowly slumped to the floor.

Pax let go of him. He straightened himself back onto all four feet, watching the body on the floor for any signs of life. The injury was bad, and it should keep him down permanently, but he wasn't going to risk it until he was completely sure. More blood flowed out into the growing puddle on the floor, staining the floral rug a dark burgundy.

Finally, when he was sure there was no chance they'd ever hear from Emery Ballard again, Pax looked up at Carrie. His lungs heaved as he caught his breath, but the sight before him took it all away again. She was beautiful, as she always was, but something had changed in her. No, it was in the way she looked at him. He'd seen curiosity in her eyes as he talked about logging, and awe when he showed her a project he'd finished. There'd been warmth and longing, even when she tried to hide it.

Now, there was only contempt.

17

Thunder pounded through her. No, not thunder. It wasn't even the horrid crashing, splintering, and violent roaring that'd taken place just a moment ago. It was her heart hammering against her ribcage and echoing against the inside of her skull. What she'd seen was utterly impossible. Carrie swallowed, though her throat was completely dry. She took stock of her body to see if this was real or if she'd simply dreamed it. Her left arm was sore where Emery had pressed it against her body, and both of her wrists hurt from him twisting them behind her back. The pain in her right hand was very real, though she wouldn't hesitate if she ever needed to stab someone with her favorite pen again. It had turned into a rather handy tool, one that had done more damage than she'd imagined it to be capable of. Her entire body was shaking. All of that was proof that what had just happened was absolutely real.

But there was a bear standing in the corner of her office. Carrie lifted her eyes to it, seeing that it was also watching her. No, not *it*. *Him*. It was Pax. She knew the mind was a powerful thing, a tool that could create all sorts of wild scenarios, but she hadn't imagined him barging into her office at just the moment she needed him and...turning into a bear.

And now, as though she hadn't been through enough, he began the transformation into the Pax she'd come to know over the last couple of weeks. The shaggy fur all over his body receded, leaving just the graying sandy blonde hair on his head and forearms. The heavy, muscular body of a wild animal shrunk and changed—painfully, according to the look on his face—into that of a human. He was still strong, but in a different way now than he'd been when he'd sliced Emery's throat. The beast straightened onto two feet as the wide paws returned to capable hands, ones that she'd seen wield tools to build and create instead of destroy. Even his eyes were different. As a bear, they were dark and deep, even darker than those of the other bear. With a swirl of color, they were that sapphire blue again, a shade she'd come to admire.

She had no idea what to think about it now.

"Carrie." His voice was surprisingly human, though she somehow expected it to come out as some brutish roar. He took a slow step toward her and then another. "Are you all right?"

There wasn't a single part of her body that didn't hurt after struggling to evade Emery, but it was a different pain altogether that she noticed the most. "How can you ask me that?" Her voice was hoarse, barely above a whisper. She realized her throat was raw from screaming.

The way his eyes turned down a little at the outer corners had always given him a bit of a soulful look, but now it made him look utterly sorrowful. "I'm sorry. Why don't we go out into the living room and talk?" Pax bent and held out a hand to help her up.

Carrie examined it doubtfully. There was no sign of the bear paw it'd so recently been. He had wide flat palms, strong fingers, and several callouses. She could even see the lines that crisscrossed his palm and the whirl of his fingerprints, but how could she ever forget that long, thick bear claws waited just under the surface?

Stubbornly, Carrie pushed her hands against the floor and stood without his assistance. "I've got it, thanks." She paused, seeing that he'd positioned himself between her and the door. Carrie had already turned her back on one person who was apparently more than he seemed, and now he lay dead on the floor. Pax had saved her from that fate, but who would save her from him?

Seeing that she wasn't going anywhere, Pax moved away first. He stepped out into the dining room, checking over his shoulder to see that she was coming with him before he moved on into the living room.

Her stomach churned. Her entire body hounded her to just curl up and go to sleep, and maybe she'd wake up in the morning to find out that it'd been nothing more than a nightmare. There was too much evidence to suggest otherwise, though. Putting one foot in front of the other, she slowly made her way out into the living room.

He waited for her near the fireplace. How ironic that they would talk there, right where their bodies had made it so clear what they wanted. Maybe it was just as well. If he was going to shatter everything she thought she felt for him, he might as well do it all the way. "What...the hell...was that?" she managed to grind out as she sank into a chair.

"Carrie, I..." Pax trailed off, looking helpless. He flicked the pad of his thumb against the edge of the mantel for a moment. "I know I have a lot to explain. This isn't how I wanted you to find out."

"I'm not even sure *what* it is that I just found out," she retorted. Her fear was making her angry. Carrie could keep her composure while she listened to other people fight and hash out all the little arguments that made them miserable in their marriages, but this was something she'd never even come close to dealing with before. "Did I actually see that? Or am I going crazy?"

"You're not crazy," he said quickly. "I'm a shifter, Carrie. I can change from human to bear any time I want to. As you know now from what you just saw in there, I'm not the only one. There are a lot of us."

Hearing him say it out loud didn't make it any less overwhelming. She pressed her palm against her forehead. The whole world was spinning around her, and she just wanted it to stop. "When were you going to tell me this? Or did you plan to at all?" How long might she have gone on without knowing who this man really was?

"Actually, I was going to tell you today, among other things. It's not an easy secret to tell."

"Until there's a dead bear on my office floor," she choked out. Carrie leaned forward, bracing her elbows on her knees. It wasn't enough. She clutched her stomach as she bent as far as the chair would let her. She thought she would be sick, but she'd much rather have the flu than be going through this.

He was crouched in front of her in a moment. "I'm sorry, Carrie. For everything. I know it's a lot to handle. I'm not sure I could even tell you all of it in one night. There's too much. This isn't how I planned for it to go, but I guess it'll serve as a start if it has to." His fingers touched the backs of her arms, and then his palms spread out over her upper back. They were warm and comforting.

It was exactly what she *didn't* want from him right now. Carrie reeled upright in her chair, scooting it away from him. "A start? You think a *start* is you killing a man? With your bare...claws?" She could hear how crazy she sounded, but she didn't care anymore. The whole thing *was* crazy.

"He was going to kill *you*," Pax reminded her. "It's not as though I had a choice."

"But I guess you did out in the woods," she muttered, feeling more miserable than ever as she stared down into those eyes. She, of all people, understood that it took some time to get to know a person, to dig down past the façade they put up when they wanted to impress you and find the truth of their soul. There were always going to be some flaws, but this was something she just couldn't comprehend. She tried to focus on the fact as much as possible. "That was him out there last week, wasn't it?"

"Yes." Seeing that she wasn't interested in any comfort from him, Pax stood. "And it was me, too."

"And I was dumb enough not to realize it." A sob thickened her voice.

"Not dumb," he corrected. "There was no reason for you to think otherwise."

She supposed there was some truth to that. Carrie felt the desperate need to sort this out, to put everything into neat categories in her brain so she could understand it. The information simply refused to make sense. "All my life, I've gone around thinking that humans were simply humans. Now I'm finding that it was a lie. Everything was. Everything with you..." Her chest constricted.

"No. No, that's not true." Pax moved toward her, this time kneeling beside her chair. He grabbed her hand and held it in his. "Nothing else was a lie. Nothing else that could ever be between us—"

"Stop it." She swallowed. Her face was swelling up from all the tears. Carrie was sure she looked like a horrid mess, but she couldn't remember ever crying this hard. The emotional roller coaster she'd been on that day was too much to handle, yet she had no choice. "Just stop it right now. Don't talk to me about anything that was between us. You can't just march into someone's life and act like everything is completely normal when there's something this big happening. You can't expect me to be all right with it."

Pax squeezed her fingers gently. His eyes pleaded with her. "Carrie, please. I know it's a mess. I do. I just need you to accept that this is something I can't simply tell people about."

"Accept?" She yanked her hand out of his grip. "Don't ask me to accept any of this!"

His fingers curled into the upholstery on the arm of the chair. He let go as he stood, fast enough that it made her jump a little inside. But he moved away from her and toward the window, rubbing one hand against the back of his neck. Finally, he turned his head back toward her so she could see his profile. "Isn't that what your book is all about? Accepting your partner for who they really are and finding ways to make that work for the couple?"

Her blood curdled with anger. It gave her the strength she needed to get on her feet again. "Don't you dare use my words against me!"

Pax had been apologetic, but now she could see the anger simmering in his eyes as well. "But isn't it?" he challenged. "You talk all about how you can't change another person, how you have to learn to live with them as they are."

"Yes, as long as they do the same for you!" she retorted. "It's not like you had much consideration for me, or else you would've told me already!"

His hands bunched into fists at his sides, but Carrie knew he wouldn't hurt her. All the damage he could do had already been done. "You're not thinking about this, Carrie. How could you expect me to just blurt out that I'm a fucking bear? You'd think I was nuts, and then you'd never speak to me again!"

"I guess that would've been for the best then, huh?" The pain that rippled through her heart was almost unbearable. To think that she'd been seriously considering what possibilities there might be for their future. She'd been alone for so long, thinking only about what was best for her children instead of anything she wanted for herself, and as soon as she'd thought about letting someone in, he happened to be a shifter. "I don't even know why we're talking about this like we need some sort of therapy when we don't have a relationship! You work on my house, and I pay you, and that's it! I'm not going to delude myself any longer into thinking there could be more than that!"

Pax's jaw tightened. He looked like he was having a hard time keeping control of himself. He took a deep breath and forced his fingers to straighten. "This isn't a good time for us to be talking about this. You've just had a bad scare and some big news. I'm going to call a couple of people and take care of Emery. You go upstairs and lay down for a bit."

He was taking charge, just like he'd already done for her twice. There were times when Carrie had enjoyed that, but right now, it only pissed her off more. "I don't need you to tell me what to do."

"Would you rather I just leave?" He flung his hand toward the front door.

Yes. Yes, she absolutely wanted him to leave. She wanted him to walk out that door, dragging her heart down the porch steps behind him, and never come back again. She wanted to beat her fists against his chest for being so damned likable and sweet and wonderful and horrible. She wanted to slump down on the floor and press her hands against her heart and cry like she'd never cried before.

But she couldn't exactly let him go while there was still some not-quite-human creature in her office, and there was no getting around that, no matter how upset she was. "Just...do what you need to do and then get the hell out of my life." She turned and marched up the stairs, telling herself that she was doing it because she wanted to and not because he told her to.

Her hand grazed the railing, solid and smooth. Carrie snatched her hand back as though she'd just touched fire. Another sob pushed up through her throat, and the stairs blurred in her vision. How could this be so hard? She'd seen it a thousand times. Acceptance and understanding were important, but some things were simply unforgivable.

Everything was wrong. Everything was so unbelievably wrong. Her feet hit the landing and carried her into her bedroom. Carrie slammed the door behind her. She'd have to slam the door on any future with Pax, too. Slumping down on the bed, she let her tears fall. They showered her cheeks and dripped down onto her lap. She'd been stupid enough to let herself fall into his arms on that first night, and she'd been blinded to everything else ever since then. He'd lied to her, and now there was no way of telling just how many times.

He'd also protected her. If she tried, she could still feel the warmth of his arms when he wrapped them around her. She could see the horror and fury in his eyes when he found Emery holding his knife to her throat.

But those images of him as a bear simply wouldn't leave her alone.

18

"Thanks," Pax grunted into the silent air of the truck cab.

Chase wiped his hands on a rag and tossed it onto the floorboard. "You're welcome. I'm flattered that you think of me when you need help, but I have to admit, I'd much rather deal with kitchen cabinets or flooring than a dead body."

"You and me both." Pax felt as though all eyes were on him as he headed through town. The hulking figure they'd loaded into the truck bed was covered with a tarp and strapped down. No one would think a thing of it, but he was very aware of just what it was he was hauling.

"Pax, if you're worried about what Chris is going to say, I'd let it go. He's not going to be pleased because he's got to take care of it, but you were in the right here. You said this douche was threatening Carrie. It's not like you had a choice."

"No." He sure as hell didn't, and that was exactly what made it so frustrating. "I had to kill him. If I'd let him go, he would've come right back for her and God knows who else."

"So we're good," Chase concluded.

"When it comes to that, sure. But not Carrie." Pax stared at the traffic light in the middle of town, willing it to change. "Not at all."

"Uh oh. I guess that means she wasn't all that excited to find out the truth. Just give her some time. Jenna was freaked out, too, but she came around. She'll get past it."

"I don't know about that." Her haunted eyes lingered in his mind. "I think she was angrier that I hadn't told her. I don't think she's going to see me again."

"It's a lot to unpack. Maybe I can send Jenna over there and—"

"No." Pax cut that idea off before it could turn into anything more. "I already told her my secret, and because of Emery, I had to admit that there are others. But that's no reason to drag you and Jenna into it. This is just proof of exactly why I can't be with a human. They don't understand."

Chase shifted in his seat. "You can't lump them all together like that."

"They do it to us!" Pax slammed his palm into the steering wheel. "They find out we're not like them, and they freak the fuck out! We're lucky they haven't turned it into some witch hunt, with all the humans trying to figure out how to tell who's an animal and who isn't. What happens if we tell the wrong person?"

"Hey!" Chase put his hand out. "Chill out, man. I know it's hard. I know you're upset. You have every right to be, considering what you just went through. But you told me just a few days ago that you were pretty sure Carrie was your mate. If that's true, then she's going to come around. She'll get past this, and so will you."

Pax let out a dry laugh that had no humor behind it. "You have a ridiculously positive attitude for someone who's helping to hide a dead guy."

"Hey, I do what I can."

They were heading out from the other side of town now, and Pax turned onto the twisting roads that would take them to their Alpha's house. He was glad. He just wanted to get this over with. He tightened his grip on the steering wheel, feeling even more unsettled than he had for the last couple of weeks. "I was going to tell her."

"Hm?"

"That's why I went over there today and why I happened to get there just in time to save her. We'd finished logging for the day, and I decided just to head over and tell her how I felt. The rest of it—shifting and all that—would have to come later, but I was going to tell her." He let a long breath out through his nose, remembering the way she'd looked down at him from that chair. "Once we didn't have to worry about our lives being in danger anymore, I tried to talk to her. She didn't want to hear any of it."

"I'm sorry, man."

He was sorry, too. Sorry that he'd let himself think it was time to settle down with a mate, and doubly sorry that he let himself believe it could be her.

They reached Chris's place and pulled up the driveway. Pax had already called, and Chris and his brother Tyler were waiting on the front porch.

"Any witnesses?" Chris asked as he stepped up to the side of the truck. He peered in with a disgusted look on his face.

"Just Carrie O'Connor, the human I told you about." Pax unfastened the straps that held down the tarp. Yes, he'd told Chris about Carrie, but not the details that mattered. She was just a woman he was doing some work for.

The Alpha glanced over the body before nodding for Pax to put the tarp back in place. "Is she going to tell anyone?"

"No." Pax hadn't told her explicitly to keep their secret. There was no need. She was angry about the knowledge and probably somewhat traumatized by it, but he was fairly certain he had nothing to worry about. "She won't."

Tyler swept a hand through the buzzed sides of his hair. "I guess it's finally time to have an official meeting with the Ballards. This is proof enough that they've been messing with our operations."

Pax jutted his chin toward Emery. "He was trying to get Carrie to tell him where our next logging contracts were going to be. He'd been watching me, and he knew I was at her house a lot. He assumed the two of us were dating and that she knew my business. He didn't realize I was just there for work. Anyway, I'd say they sent him in to get some better information so they could completely sabotage an entire contract for us instead of just compromising some equipment." It pissed him off all over again to know that Emery and his other clan members were likely responsible for the broken hydraulic hose and the truckload of logs that'd nearly killed Dean.

Chris nodded. "Let's get him in the back of my truck, and then I'll take him straight to Jacob Ballard himself. He's not going to be very happy when I throw a dead body on his doorstep, but I think he'll take the hint."

"It could mean an all-out war," Tyler warned. "Considering how long the Ballards have been trying to get at us, I wouldn't be surprised if they tried to turn around and use this against us even though they were the instigators."

"They always have been," his brother agreed. Chris shook his head. "I'd much rather have peace around here, but I'll do what it takes to get them to back off. We need to make sure our more vulnerable members are protected before I go over there. Tyler, start working through the list of everyone who lives on their own, especially the elderly. If we can get them to stay here where we've got some security, we'll gladly open the house to them. I'll warn Brandy that we might be having some house guests."

"What can I do?" Pax stepped forward, ready to take some sort of action that would bring this nasty fight to a close. He already felt like it had ruined his life.

Chris gestured for Tyler, Chase, and the few others who'd filtered out of the house to take care of the body. He grabbed Pax by the arm and led him in the other direction, closer to the front door. "There's only one thing I need you to do, and I think you know exactly what it is."

Pax was an active member of the clan. He came to all the meetings and kept up with what was going on. He was even related to the Alpha as a fellow Thompson, but now he looked at him in confusion. "I don't, actually."

"Get back to Carrie's house."

The words hit him hard, slapping him in the face. He'd already done enough damage over there. "I don't think that's a good idea."

Chris's dark red hair was several shades lighter out there in the sun, and he scratched it just above his ear. "I didn't ask what you thought."

This was a change of pace from the usual. Chris was the sort of Alpha who usually checked with the clan members, polling them for their opinion on what mattered most. "Look, if you're worried that Carrie needs protection, maybe we can arrange for it a different way. Tyler could drive by. Or she knows

Jenna. We could ask her to set up a lunch date or something."

One corner of Chris's mouth tipped up, but the amusement didn't reach his eyes. "We both know what's going on here. The main issue might be the Ballards and their beef with us, but every time I turn around, I'm hearing about you and this Carrie woman."

Pax shook his head. "This doesn't have anything to do with her or with me personally."

"Not when it comes to clan politics, no," Chris admitted. "But James told me he initially blamed you for Dean's near-death experience because of all the time you've been spending with this woman. Then I hear about you encountering a Ballard out in the woods—while you're out with the very same woman. Now they've come after her directly, and if you hadn't gone over there, we might be dealing with a dead human instead of a dead shifter."

"Like I said, if you're worried about someone coming after her, then I'm sure we can get someone to do a detail over there, sit in front of her house, and—"

"Pax." Chris grabbed him by the shoulder, his deep blue eyes staring into his. "Knock it off. Quit pretending. You're the only one who's buying this story you're trying so hard to sell. I can see what's happening."

Pax opened his mouth to protest, but a stern look from his Alpha made his bear retreat. "She doesn't want me there."

"It might seem that way," Chris admitted. "I only know the basics of what went down today at her place, and I'm sure she's rattled. But something is clearly happening between the two of you. Use your work as an excuse all you want, but you wouldn't be spending *that* much time with her if this was just for a little extra cash on the side. You make good money logging, and you know the clan is always here to take care of you. All of it is just an excuse."

He clenched his teeth. Pax didn't like being called out on such a thing. "I can see how it must look, but you don't know how pissed off she is. She told me to get the hell out of her life. She doesn't want to see me anymore, and I don't think even a threat to her life is going to change that."

Chris tipped his head slightly to the side as he studied Pax, looking like a father trying to keep his patience even though they were roughly the same age. "She's your mate, isn't she?"

"I thought so." The wound just wouldn't stop getting ripped open. He couldn't get away from it.

"Right." Chris nodded. "I don't care if she's human. We can deal with that. You're going to Carrie's house because I told you to. No matter what Carrie might've said when she was angry, she wants you, and she needs you to be there."

More arguments surfaced on the back of Pax's tongue, but he swallowed them. Chris wasn't going to hear them out. He was a good leader, and a respectful member didn't argue with his Alpha. He'd already stepped out of line far enough. "Okay."

"Good man. I'll keep you posted on how things go with the Ballards. I'm happy to let Carrie stay in her own home for the moment, but if things go sideways, you may have to bring her back here. Whether she likes it or not," he added with a grin.

Pax didn't say another word. He obediently trudged back to his now-empty truck. Chase was diving in to help Tyler and the others round up the clan, so he was free to drive back to the other side of town alone.

His mind was constantly swiveling back and forth on what he should do about Carrie. He wanted to go to her, which made it so hard to argue with Chris. He longed to drive back over there, to stomp up on the porch, fling the door open, and tell her to sit because they were going to talk. His bear seemed satisfied that Pax would be returning to Carrie's house, but he knew it wouldn't do any good.

Carrie would reject him again, and he'd be left knowing that the only person he loved hated him for who he was.

19

Carrie opened her office door and peeked inside. The place was a complete wreck, just as she knew it would be. The broken furniture and bloodstains made her stomach roll, but at least the body was gone just as Pax promised it would be. Gingerly, she moved to the other side of the room just long enough to ensure the door and windows were locked. She paused to grab her laptop and a few files, but she didn't want to be in there any longer than she had to. The skin on the back of her neck prickled as she bolted back across the room, then shut and locked the door behind her. She didn't even want to lean against it. Hopefully, at some point, she'd be able to go back in there again. But not today.

The rest of the house was not just empty but hollow. Carrie had been living alone for a while now that her kids had moved off to college, but somehow she felt more alone than on that first night with an empty nest. A chill had settled into the air and into her bones. She went to the kitchen with vague thoughts of making hot tea or coffee, but the room only made her think of Pax and the beautiful cabinets he'd promised.

With her shoulders sagging, she turned and wandered toward the living room. The fireplace glared at her, reminding her of exactly where this connection to Pax had both started and ended. They'd made love there, and Carrie knew it was something more than just physical. She'd joined with him in a way she'd never had with anyone else, yet she hadn't managed to tell him just how she'd felt. Her doubts had clouded her mind, and it was only as she'd sat there rejecting him that she saw his love for her in his eyes so clearly.

Feeling like she had no place to go within her own house and too uncertain about going anywhere else, Carrie sank onto the stairs. She needed something to do. Her sobbing session upstairs had been cathartic, and she was surprised that it hadn't exhausted her to the point of sleep. Setting her laptop down next to her, she began flipping through her files. When she'd first opened her practice, Carrie made a habit to read over her client notes regularly. She never wanted someone to come in for an appointment and feel as though she hadn't taken the time to get to know them.

"Focus," she whispered to herself as she opened the first file and felt like she might as well be reading a foreign language. "This is your job, and it doesn't matter if you have your own personal struggles." But the client files were just laughing in her face. She'd told the Goodalls that they weren't communicating with each other enough. Then there were the Monroes, who needed to live in each other's shoes for a while. The Kurlanders needed more patience, because good things didn't always happen instantly or easily.

Acceptance. They all needed acceptance of the things they couldn't change, because no one was perfect.

Carrie dashed her files to the side and lay back on the stairs. There was an entire chapter about how even the perfect partner probably wasn't a perfect person in her book. Who was she to be smiling on the back cover and touting such bullshit when she clearly didn't follow it herself?

Pax was calm and kind. Smart and capable. Being incredibly gorgeous didn't hurt either. He could be the classic, protective male, but he also let her make her own decisions. He was the entire package, the type of man that every woman wanted. He just happened to be a bear, too.

A sigh escaped her lips. She didn't think of herself as someone who needed rescuing, but now she wondered who would come along and rescue her when she truly needed it. Pax had fallen easily—and seemingly happily—into that category, but she wouldn't be seeing him again for a long time. Carrie let her eyes wander along the ceiling, trying to find the love she'd had for this house when she'd decided to buy it, but her gaze landed on something she'd never noticed before.

It was on the underside of the new railing Pax had installed, a piece of him that was also a part of her. The wood beneath the was smooth and finegrained, but it was marred just before it joined with the newel post. Carrie sat up to get a better look at it. The initials P.T. and C.C. were carved inside a heart. It was small, much smaller than the one they'd found out in the forest, but sized perfectly to be tucked away from view.

Her heart sank into her stomach, through the

floor, and toward the center of the Earth. He loved her. She traced the outline of the heart with her finger, envisioning what he must have looked like as he sat right where she was sitting and engraved his love for her into the wood.

A heavy pounding sounded on the door, just across from where she sat. "Carrie?"

Pax's voice pulsed through her soul.

"Carrie?" He knocked again. "It's me."

She glanced down at the discarded client files and knew she'd been letting herself think about this too much. There was a time and a place for calm logic when it came to creating and deepening a relationship, but if she'd gone with her instincts in the first place, they might not be in this situation. Carrie let go of her imposter syndrome, her fear of whether or not she'd be in a successful relationship again, and even her fear of the wild animal that lived inside the man she loved. She let her body take over as it stood and crossed the room to open the door.

He stepped in as soon as the latch opened, closing the door behind him and locking it. He kept his eyes on what he was doing instead of on her. "I'm sure you don't want to see me right now, but I don't have much choice. I need to be here in case one of Emery's relatives decides to come after you."

Finally, those deep midnight eyes met hers. They burrowed into her very core, and she melted at the pure despair they held. People looked to her for help and advice, but Pax simply wanted her. "I'm sorry I—"

"I'm really sorry about—" he started at the same time.

Carrie smiled a little. Her entire body longed with a need for him. He was right there, so close, yet she felt as though she'd pushed herself miles away when she'd gotten angry with him. "If you'd like to talk—"

"—talk about things—"

If they kept saying the same things at the same time, they weren't going to get anywhere. But it made her hope that the other thing she wanted was exactly what he wanted, too. Carrie could feel the energy between them, the distance expanding and contracting as their chests heaved with anticipation. She closed that distance, pressing her lips to his and kissing him for all she was worth. If he didn't want her, then at least she'd know she tried.

But Pax's hands closed around her hips and pulled her close. His lips responded, warm and soft, demanding, yet so generous. She slipped her tongue between them, rewarded with a deep groan of pleasure that made her nipples harden. Wrapping her arms around his neck and letting her fingers play in the freshly trimmed hair on the back of his head, she thought she could stay there forever, just kissing him. He pulled back, though, breaking their lip lock and making her ache for him even as he kept her in his arms.

She felt desperation wash over her again as she moved her head back just enough that she could look into his eyes. "I don't expect you to forgive me, Pax, but I'm so incredibly sorry. You were right. About everything."

His hand skimmed along her lower back, his finger slipping inside the back belt loop of her jeans. "You don't have anything to be sorry for. I should've told you before."

Carrie laughed a little, delighted simply to feel this close to him. "I can't blame you for that. It's a big part of your life."

"That's true, but I'd like you to be a big part of it, too. I love you, Carrie."

A thrill unlike any she'd known before rippled through her body. "I love you, too." She kissed him again.

Pax scooped his hands underneath her backside and lifted her easily off the floor and into his arms.

"Care to make it official?" He headed toward the stairs.

Carrie got a heady feeling as he began the ascent, and it only grew when she reached out and trailed her fingers along the handrail. She burrowed her face into his neck, inhaling the scents of cedar and pine. Her body relaxed, but she wasn't tired.

He bumped the bedroom door open with his hip, and the two of them tumbled onto the bed as he kissed her again, his lips luxurious against hers. He trailed them down her throat and around the side of her neck as his fingers nimbly slipped the buttons on her blouse free. Warm, rough hands edged under the material and around her back to find her bra's clasp.

Carrie gasped a little as he freed her, surprised at how good it felt to get rid of her clothes in front of him. Her body wasn't the same as it used to be, and other men might have made her feel self-conscious, but with Pax, she only felt sparks of delight over her skin where he touched it. She pulled at his jacket and his shirt, her skin pleading to have more of his against it.

He gave her exactly what she wanted as he shimmied her jeans down. He grazed his hands over her feminine hips and then squeezed, worshiping the generous curves. The frenzy with which they'd been moving slowed as he leaned back to drink in the sight of her. Those remarkable eyes drifted over her breasts, and then his mouth joined them. His tongue was hot and wet as it caressed her nipple, his movement passionate and determined.

Carrie wrapped her body around his. Her head tipped back and she closed her eyes, focusing only on the way it felt to have someone love her. Pax's adorations left a tangle of pleasure in the pit of her stomach and sent magnificent trembling through her limbs. She started to open her eyes when his kisses stopped, but then she felt the gentle stroke of his finger further down.

He caressed the insides of her thighs, bringing back memories of the way he'd pleased her on the night they met. But then his heated lips pressed sultry kisses between her legs. Her breath left her lungs as Pax built the tension inside her, crafting something as exquisite and achingly beautiful as his woodwork, his tongue languorously tracing her folds and finding where it was most useful. Plundering her with his mouth, Pax sent bursts of dizziness and pleasure through her body. They converged and erupted when he pushed her past that edge as she twisted her hands in the sheets and called out his name.

Dazed, Carrie took a moment to catch her breath as Pax stood, freeing himself from his jeans. Her desire for him swelled as she saw that he was ready for her, his shaft hard against the dusting of hair and his muscled thighs. His eyes were luminous with his hunger for her, and she twined her legs around him as he came back down onto the bed. His length was hot and heavy against her, throbbing against that most sensitive spot that he'd just pleasured. Carrie craved another round of satisfaction, one that was much deeper. She'd waited long enough to have him again, wasting time. She rolled her hips against his to entice him.

Pax obliged, his tip resting against her for a moment before plunging inside. Simply having him inside her was enough to rev her up again. Carrie felt her temperature rising as she became slick around him. She raked her fingers over his shoulder blades and pressed her palms down either side of his spine. Feeling the last of her inhibitions fly free, she reached down a little further and squeezed his firm ass.

Pax was getting harder inside her, filling and fulfilling her. For once, Carrie wasn't thinking about the consequences of being with someone or the 'right' things to do within that relationship. She couldn't completely forget about the fact that he was a bear, because she swore she could sense it in his soul. It was the hot, animalistic side of him, a part of him that she'd fallen in love with before she even understood it existed. Being with Pax was exciting and new, yet familiar, and her heart soared in knowing that he loved her.

His hips drove harder, grinding against her and bringing them both closer to that fantastic, final sweetness. Carrie thrust back, and the coiled spring inside her exploded once again as he clutched her tightly and filled her with his love.

20

"Welcome to Two Birches Bed and Breakfast! Feel free to have a look around, and don't hesitate to ask if you have any questions. Help yourself to the refreshments in the kitchen."

Pax watched as Carrie cheerfully greeted the guests at the open house and showed them around. The house had taken a long time and a hell of a lot of work to remodel, but it was stunning. It was all the more beautiful because he knew he and Carrie had a shared history there.

He came up behind his mate and put his hand on her lower back as she rejoined the rest of his clan that had arrived to show their support. "You're doing great, honey."

"I have to agree." Jenna held Alexander on her

hip, smiling warmly at him as he played with the buttons on her shirt. "I don't think you even needed any help from me."

"That's not true," Carrie argued with a smile. "I've already gotten some interest in the couples' package for people who want to stay here and have a few therapy sessions. That website you built me for bookings will be a complete lifesaver. It wouldn't be what it is at all without you. And without Pax, of course."

"He does know his way around the woodshop." Dean raised a beer, and Evan clanked his against it. "I guess that makes it worth all the time he's been spending away from his chainsaw, but don't get used to it. James is going to be cranky if you take any more vacation time."

"You don't have to worry about that," Pax replied. "I just wanted to make sure I got the last few things finished up, and then it'll all go back to normal. Carrie and I will still work our current jobs, but we figure we can squeeze the B&B in around everything else."

Chris and Brandy arrived just then, each of them holding one of little Edwin's hands to keep the future Alpha from getting into anything. Tyler and Liz tagged along behind them, only holding each other's hands. The Alpha clapped Pax on the shoulder before turning a warm smile to Carrie. "We had to come and congratulate you on your grand opening, but there's something else we'd like to tell you."

Carrie glanced at Pax uncertainly before nodding for Chris to go on.

"It pains me to say it, I admit, but we took your advice when it came to the Ballards. We asked them to sit and talk with us, with no threat of retaliation for their sabotage or for trying to come after you. I really would've rather sliced a few of them open," he added quietly, "but we just talked. We discussed all the problems that our two clans have been having over the years, which go back pretty far. Once we laid it all out on the table, both Jacob and I decided that the violence and anger couldn't go on any longer. We agreed to put our old feud to rest before anyone else gets hurt."

"Really?" Carrie's green eyes widened with excitement.

"Believe it or not," Brandy said, poking her mate in the shoulder teasingly. "At first, I thought they were just going to start throwing their fists at each other. But Chris had the foresight to bring me along, and Jacob's mate Eloise was there as well. She and I started talking about everything from babies to pie recipes, the way moms do, and I think it helped smooth the path for them to talk instead of beating each other."

"That's wonderful," Carrie replied genuinely. "I can't tell you how happy I am to hear that. Could you please excuse me for a minute? I've got a few more guests arriving." She brushed her hand across Pax's as she moved back to the front door.

"She's really digging this, huh?" Chase asked, nudging Pax with his elbow.

Carrie was greeting Dane Morris, the former owner who'd shown up to see what they'd done with the place. He had his hands tucked in the front pockets of his old Levi's as Carrie talked to him, but he was nodding enthusiastically.

"She was determined to do it, and she made it happen. After our incident with Emery, I was worried she might give up and want to move, but it only drove her harder. Any time she hasn't been with her clients, she's been sanding and staining and painting right alongside me." Carrie could be patient, calm, and cerebral, but could also shout expletives at a rusty door hinge when she got frustrated with a screw that wouldn't come loose.

Chase nodded. "So I was right."

"Hm?"

"That you needed to tell her how you felt," his cousin goaded. "The two of you are the talk of the clan, you know. Only in a good way," he amended. "Apparently, there were quite a few members who figured you'd never settle down, but now they think it's charming and sweet how in love you are."

"Shut up." Pax's cheeks burned at the idea of anyone talking about him that much, though he would've endured a thousand rumors if it meant he got to be with Carrie. "Hey, isn't that your real estate agent?" He pointed across the room, where a woman in a blue blazer had just walked in and began gushing to Carrie about how amazing the place was.

"I think everyone in town is interested in seeing it," Chase said with a nod. "What about these two? You know them?"

Pax looked. The guy was only vaguely familiar, but there was no mistaking the woman. He let out a little laugh. "That's Sophie. She was at the speed dating event, the one I told you about when I met Carrie. I think he was there, too. In fact, if I remember correctly, they left together. I'm surprised they're still dating. I didn't think he'd be her type." Sophie had interrupted Carrie's conversation and was going on and on about the place, running her hands down her date's arms every now and then as he gazed at her adoringly.

"You never know who your type might be, am I right?" He elbowed Pax again.

"You're never going to let me live this down, are you?"

"That I was right and you were wrong?" Chase tipped his head to the side as though he were thinking. "Not a chance."

Just then, Carrie clapped her hands to get everyone's attention. "Ladies and gentlemen, I can't thank you enough for coming out here tonight. It's meant so much to us to see that the community is as excited about Two Birches as we are." She paused for a moment while a round of applause rippled through the room. "I'm extremely happy to announce that we have our very first guests booked! Sophie McCall and her fiancé, Richard Bellington!"

Sophie and Richard waved and smiled like they were celebrities. Pax was stunned, but it just proved the point that all different kinds of people could fall in love.

His phone buzzed. Pax checked his message and smiled. "It's almost time. Will you get the door?"

Chase grinned, having been filled in on the secret earlier. "You bet. Just tell me when."

Pax came up behind Carrie just as she finished chatting with a couple of clients who headed upstairs to check out the bedrooms. "You've taken to clan life pretty well. You know, for a human."

"Pfft!" She slapped his arm playfully, her eyes dancing. "It's nothing like I ever expected, but I love it. I do have to admit I keep finding myself watching the other couples. I'm fascinated to know what makes them fated to each other and no one else."

"Always the therapist," he said as he leaned in to kiss her. Carrie's lips were warm and pleasant, making him temporarily forget what he was supposed to be doing. "The only thing that matters is that you're mine. Although if you really want to dig down and study it, you should know that sometimes a shifter will go out of his way to surprise his mate just to show her how much he loves her."

"He will?" Her eyes glittered as she watched him curiously. "And here I thought he already showed her that by helping her build a beautiful house and business."

"It's a start, but there will always be more." Pax turned and gave the nod to Chase.

He opened the door to reveal two kids in their late teens. The girl had long dark hair, while the boy's was combed back to control his curls, but they both had the same bright green eyes.

"Cam! Cat!" Carrie screamed as she charged across the room to hug her children. "How did this happen? I didn't think you could come up! You had schoolwork, and the drive was going to take way too long!"

"There's a lot you can get done on a plane with a laptop," Cat replied, giving her mom an extra squeeze.

Carrie shook her head. "But you can't afford plane tickets! You should have asked me."

Cam bobbed his head toward Pax. "We had a little help, and there was no way we were going to miss your grand opening."

"Oh, my gosh." Carrie stepped back to look at her two children and Pax. "I just can't believe this. You've all made this the happiest day of my life."

"How about you give them the grand tour?" Pax suggested.

For the next twenty minutes, he happily followed along as Carrie went over every detail of the house with her twins. They oohed and aahed appropriately at the custom handrail, the new kitchen cabinets, and even the original trim that'd been salvaged from the old shed out back and put in the bedrooms upstairs. He didn't argue as Carrie tried to give him credit for everything, but he made a mental note to go back and tell Cat and Cam just how much hard work their mom had put in as well.

Eventually, when Carrie had calmed down a little from her initial excitement and they'd come back downstairs, he couldn't wait any longer. "I have another surprise for you."

"As if I needed any more."

"Can we step inside your office?"

They introduced the twins to Jenna and Liz, who took them into the kitchen to fill them up with as much food as they could handle.

Pax shut the door behind him on the newly remodeled office. He'd personally ripped everything out of there that might've given Carrie any reminder of what had happened. It still smelled like fresh paint and new stain, and she'd picked a comforting shade of sage green for the walls.

"I can't thank you enough," she said, shaking her head. "Having them here, and you here…it's like having my family back together."

He nodded. "That's what I was hoping for. I chatted with them a bit on the phone as we were making the arrangements. They seem like great kids, and they absolutely love you. I do, too, and that's why I wanted to give you this." Pax reached behind him for the small box he'd tucked away on the bookshelf.

There was no evidence of that hard shell he'd noticed on Carrie when they first met. It had melted away, letting all her love and light shine. Pax was thrilled he had the chance to bask in it. He'd wasted enough time telling her how he felt, and now he'd vowed to himself that he'd never stop showing her his love.

"A new pen!" She lifted the fountain pen carefully out of the box, looking at it curiously. "Is it made of wood?"

"From the same tree that we cut down for the railing," he admitted. "Look at the end of the cap."

There, in tiny letters engraved with a laser, were their initials.

THE END

If you enjoyed *Bear's Midlife Matchmaker*, you'll love *Bear's Midlife Second Chance*! Read on for a preview of Dean's story.

DEAN

"Don't do that! You'll erase everything I've done!" Rebecca Miller waved her hands frantically over the keyboard. Since when did cash registers have keyboards, anyway? The damn thing was just a computer with some fancy software, and she'd thought for sure she'd been doing her parents a favor when she'd ordered it for Claire's Confections. She wasn't about to come all the way back home to Carlton, Oregon just to be handwriting receipts.

"How do you know? It's not like any of it makes sense." Her father squinted at the screen, which was much bigger than the one on Rebecca's laptop back at home. He sighed, running his hand through his dark auburn hair and knocking his toupee off-kilter in the process. "I already tried pushing every damn button on the thing!"

"Dad."

"What?"

Rebecca waved a finger around the top of her head. "Your hair?"

"Damn it," he mumbled as he attempted to straighten the rug but only made it worse.

"I thought Mom said she got this figured out. You guys have had this for a few weeks now. Mom?"

Claire Miller came to the front desk. She wasn't as spry as she used to be, and Rebecca was still getting used to seeing her as a woman in her seventies. Her shoulders were starting to hunch, and she didn't seem to have the energy she used to. She'd insisted she was still perfectly fine, but an incident with some peanuts that caused a customer to go into anaphylaxis was all the proof Rebecca needed that it was time to come home. "Yes, I got it figured out."

"Good." Rebecca stepped back and put her hands in the air. "Then show me."

"It's very simple, honey." Claire patted her daughter's cheek before she reached into the drawer. "You just take out a receipt pad and a pen, and then you completely ignore the stupid machine."

Rebecca laughed as she tucked a strand of

blonde hair that had escaped her bun behind her ear. "That's one method, Mom, but it's not going to work for much longer. We need to update this place."

"Seriously," Madison grumbled from where she slumped in a chair near the front door. She didn't even bother looking up, keeping her gaze as permanently riveted to her phone as it always was. "You don't even have Wi-Fi."

Looking up and preparing to argue, Rebecca crooked her finger at her daughter instead. "Come here, missy."

Madison rolled her eyes as she tucked her phone in the pocket of her hoodie and stood up. "What?"

"Come *all the way* around here," she specified, waving impatiently. It seemed like Madison was trying to do as little as possible these days, and her favorite hobby was irritating her mother. "I'm going to clear this all out. Now, can you ring up an order of a dozen cake pops?"

"Cake pops are so five years ago," Madison growled. She stared at the screen for a moment. Then she reached out and began poking at the screen. "You want chocolate or vanilla?"

Rebecca's mouth hung open. She hadn't even realized it was a touch screen. Her parents were both looking at the computer and their granddaughter with similar faces. "Either one."

"Okay. It's ready to take the payment. Want me to cancel it out?"

"No, no, no! I'd rather go ahead and pay for it so we can make sure this works all the way to the end. Let me just get my purse." As she headed into the back, Rebecca realized that something didn't smell right. Claire's Confections had been up and running for forty years, and Rebecca was incredibly familiar with the combined scent of sugar, chocolate, and fresh fruit. This definitely wasn't it.

She stepped into the kitchen and her heart constricted. The double boiler was on the stove, the water in the lower half bubbling over and onto the burner, sending the gas flames sparking outward. The chocolate in the top half was starting to burn, but that was the least of Carrie's concerns as she noticed the potholder nearby. Not all the flames were coming from the burner.

"Fire!" she managed to choke out after a second. Rebecca raced to the extinguisher kept on the wall, her fingers shaking as she ripped it down and began pulling at the trigger. The potholder was completely consumed in flames now, but the fire extinguisher merely spit on it.

"Shit!" Rebecca checked the dial. The damn thing was empty. She snagged her phone from her pocket and dialed 911.

"What's going on?" Madison appeared in the doorway, looking surprisingly aware of her surroundings for once.

Rebecca practically hissed through her teeth as she ran over to the sink. "Get Grandma and Grandpa out of here!" She grabbed the spray nozzle and turned it on full blast, but it wasn't quite enough to reach. The smoke alarm was ringing, and she couldn't remember hearing it start. She desperately searched for something else to throw on the flames. Something inside her told her it was time to run. She had to get the hell out of there, or she might be the next flammable target.

The fire engine screamed up the road just as Rebecca bolted out front, joining her parents and her daughter on the sidewalk. Madison had ushered her elders down to the corner, where they would be furthest from the blaze but not in the road, and she held their hands. Two men rushed into the building, dressed in full gear. Rebecca doubted they'd need that much protection, but she couldn't blame them for being cautious. After all, it wasn't as though she'd been able to do much.

"Mom, you left the stove on," she said gently. "I didn't know you were tempering chocolate when I asked you about the register."

"Was I? Oh, oh I was, wasn't I?" Realization dawned over her mother's face. She put her hands to her mouth as she glanced back at the building. "I've done it again, haven't I, Richard?"

Her husband rubbed his hand down her back. "Don't worry about it, dear. That's why we've got Rebecca here."

Rebecca's brows drew together. Things were even worse than she'd thought, and it was a good thing she came home when she did. Not that moving back to Carlton had exactly been on her bucket list, but at least she knew she was needed.

The front door burst open, and the two firemen stepped out. "Fire's extinguished now," the first one said as he took off his helmet. "There might be a little smoke damage, but it wasn't too bad."

Her lips parted as she gazed into a pair of eyes the pale shade of the noon sun. His dark hair was swept back and sweaty from his gear, and the years had changed him a little, but there was no mistaking a face so familiar. Her heart zipped up in her throat, but his name demanded to roll off her tongue.

"Dean?"

ALSO BY MEG RIPLEY
ALL AVAILABLE ON AMAZON

Shifter Nation Universe

Fated Over Forty

Book 1: Bear's Midlife Midwife

Book 2: Bear's Midlife Baby

Book 3: Bear's Midlife Matchmaker

Wild Frontier Shifters

Book 1: Her Rancher Bear

Book 2: Her Cowboy Bear

Book 3: Her Rodeo Bear

Book 4: Her Sheriff Bear

Book 5: Her Deputy Wolf

Book 6: Her Rancher Wolf

Book 7: Her Wrangler Wolf

Book 8: Her Christmas Wolf

Special Ops Shifters: L.A. Force Series

Book 1: Secret Baby For The Soldier Bear

Book 2: Saved By The Soldier Dragon

Book 3: Bonded To The Soldier Wolf

Book 4: Forbidden Mate For The Soldier Bear

Book 5: Bride For The Soldier Bear

Book 6: Feral Soldier Wolf

Book 7: Santa Soldier Bear

Special Ops Shifters: Dallas Force Series

Book 1: Rescued By The Soldier Bear

Book 2: Protected By The Soldier Tiger

Book 3: Fated To The Soldier Fox

Book 4: Baby For The Soldier Cougar

Special Ops Shifters Series (original D.C. Force)

Book 1: Daddy Soldier Bear

Book 2: Fake Mate For The Soldier Lion

Book 3: Captured By The Soldier Wolf

Book 4: Christmas With The Soldier Dragon

Werebears of Acadia Series

Werebears of the Everglades Series

Werebears of Glacier Bay Series

Werebears of Big Bend Series

Dragons of Charok Universe

Daddy Dragon Guardians Series

Shifters Between Worlds Series

More Shifter Romances

Dragon Mates: The Complete Dragons of Charok Universe Collection (Includes Daddy Dragon Guardians and Shifters Between Worlds)

Forever Fated Mates Box Set

Shifter Daddies Box Set

Beverly Hills Dragons Series

Dragons of Sin City Series

Dragons of the Darkblood Secret Society Series

Packs of the Pacific Northwest Series

Early Short Stories

Mated By The Dragon Boss

Claimed By The Werebears of Green Tree

Bearer of Secrets

Rogue Wolf

ABOUT THE AUTHOR

Meg Ripley is an author of steamy shifter romances. A Seattle native, Meg can often be found curled up in a local coffee house with her laptop.

Download Meg's entire *Caught Between Dragons* series when you sign up for her newsletter!

Sign up by visiting www.redlilypublishing.com or Meg's Facebook page:
https://www.facebook.com/authormegripley/

Lightning Source UK Ltd.
Milton Keynes UK
UKHW010744130622
404338UK00003B/139